HE HAD BACKED INTO THE STAND OF A PEANUT VENDOR.

The Bobbsey Twins at Windmill Cottage   *Frontispiece (Page 44)*

The Bobbsey Twins at Windmill Cottage

By
LAURA LEE HOPE

Author of
THE BOBBSEY TWINS SERIES

GROSSET & DUNLAP
Publishers   New York

Printed in the United States of America

The Bobbsey Twins at Windmill Cottage

CONTENTS

THE BOBBSEY TWINS
AT WINDMILL COTTAGE

CHAPTER I

THE MYSTERIOUS PACKAGE

BERT hugged the oblong package he was carrying
more firmly under his arm and jumped over the
low hedge which separated the Bobbsey garden
from that of their neighbor. In doing so he almost
fell over the kneeling figure of his sister Nan.

"Oh, hello!" cried the boy. "Couldn't see you
behind that bush. What are you doing, anyway?"

"Planting seeds, or trying to," said his twin.
She plunged her trowel into the soft earth of the
garden bed and regarded her scattered seeds rue-
fully. "You made me spill most of them and now
the flowers will grow any old way. And I do so
like a nice neat border."

"Look, Nan, forget about the seeds, won't
you?" urged Bert. "I have something much more

1

pleasant to talk to you about," he added, touching the package under his arm. "It's about this box. I don't know what to do with it."

"Who gave it to you? What's in it?" asked Nan, holding out her hand for the package.

"I got it from Mr. Jensen, the printer," Bert explained. "I happened to be passing his place when he called to me and asked if I'd mind making a delivery for him."

"Of course you said you wouldn't mind," Nan prompted. She examined the package with interest, noticing the name and address which were clearly printed on the outside wrapping.

"Of course," agreed Bert. "The funny thing about it is," he added, eyeing the girl closely to see the effect of his words, "that there is nobody living at that address!"

"Oh! Are you sure, Bert?"

"There wasn't any house at all, only an empty lot."

"That is queer," said Nan. She turned the package over and looked at it carefully. She read the address again, this time aloud. " 'Miss Hester Higgin, 22 Chester Road, Lakeport.' Why, that isn't far from here, Bert!"

"No, it should have been on my way home from Jensen's. That's why he asked me to go there, I guess. But there is no 22 Chester Road."

"Perhaps Miss Higgin lives in another house on the same street," suggested Nan.

"Maybe. But I tried the nearest ones and nobody seemed to have heard of Miss Higgin. So I came on home," Bert concluded, "and brought the package with me. The whole thing's kind of mysterious, I think."

"Yes, you're right. I'd like to see what is inside, wouldn't you?" asked Nan, looking up at her twin.

"Might be a bomb for all we know," laughed Bert. "Anyway, I guess we'd better not open it, Nan. The thing belongs to Miss Hester Higgin."

"Maybe there is no Hester Higgin," suggested Nan mysteriously. "Perhaps she is as much a—a puzzle—as the house at 22 Chester Road!"

"Oh, I guess there's such a person, all right," said Bert. "The thing is to find out where she lives."

"How are you going to do that?" Nan wanted to know.

Bert hesitated. "I might take the package back to Mr. Jensen——"

"Wait, I have a better idea!" said his twin. She jumped to her feet and started toward the house, beckoning Bert to follow. "We'll look up all the Higgins in the phone book," she explained. "If Miss Hester lives in Lakeport she should be among them."

As the older pair of Bobbsey Twins passed through the kitchen on their way to the front of the house, Nan placed the mysterious package on the kitchen table.

"I guess it will be safe enough there until we come back," she said.

"Sure," agreed Bert. "Nobody will take it."

There proved to be several families named Higgin in the telephone book. No phone was listed under the name of Hester Higgin.

"We may have to call all the numbers before we find the right one," grumbled Bert. "And we don't even know if Hester Higgin's family has a phone."

While the two children were busy with the directory, the younger twins, Flossie and Freddie, were beginning on an adventure all their own.

Through the garden door and into the kitchen came the little boy, his face flushed and his eyes shining.

"I beat you, Flossie," he shouted. "I told you I'd get home first and I did!"

"Well, you didn't beat me by very much, anyway," said his sister. "I was right behind you."

"I'm hungry," announced Freddie. "I feel as if I could eat a whole bushel of bread and strawberry jam. I wonder what that is," he added, as his eye happened to rest upon the package in the center of the kitchen table.

"Maybe there's something to eat in it," said Flossie.

"Cookies, perhaps," agreed Freddie.

The little twins stared at each other for nearly a minute, then suddenly giggled.

"Let's look!" they said together.

Freddie and Flossie pounced upon the package and began to tear the wrapping paper with their pudgy fingers. They had just cut and pulled off the cord when Dinah, the cook, came into the kitchen.

"Lan' sakes, what yo' all doin'?" exclaimed the jolly fat colored woman. "Ain't it enough for poor old Dinah to bend her bones and break her back gettin' this yere kitchen all spic and span 'thout you chilluns turnin' it upside down the minute my back's turned? Nebber did see such ones for makin' a nice clean place upside down in no time at all."

Flossie and Freddie regarded the bits of twine and pieces of torn paper that littered Dinah's spotless linoleum.

"We didn't mean to make a mess," apologized Flossie.

"We'll pick up every little piece," offered Freddie.

"You best run along outside," said Dinah, suddenly good-natured again. "When young folks starts cleanin' up seems lak' all dey makes is more mess. Shoo, now! Get along with you!"

Flossie and Freddie hurried into the garden. Under Freddie's arm, hugged tightly against his warm, chubby little person, was the mysterious oblong box.

Meanwhile Bert and Nan copied down the addresses and telephone numbers of all the Higgin families. They would call every number, if necessary, until they should find the Miss Hester Higgin to whom the package belonged.

"I'll try the first number and if that isn't right, you try the next one. We'll take turns," suggested Nan.

"All right with me," agreed Bert. "The first address is 6 Carlton Place. An Andrew Higgin lives there. Phone number is Lakeport 5486."

Nan tried it and a moment later a man's gruff voice answered.

"Yes, my name's Andrew Higgin and I live here with my wife and two daughters," he said. "But there's not a Hester among them. Never heard of the lady. Very sorry, I'm sure."

"He was *not* sorry," said Nan as she hung up the receiver. "He sounded cross as a bear at being bothered. Now you try, Bert. I'll read you the number."

Bert drew a sharp-voiced lady who declared that she had never known any one by the name of Hester.

"I wonder if all people by the name of Higgin

are bad-tempered," said Bert as he turned from the phone. "You'd think they could answer a simple question without trying to bite you. What's next, Nan?"

"There's only one more, a Mr. Samuel Higgin on Cherry Road. I'll call that number," said Nan.

"Let's hope it's the right one," Bert added.

A woman's voice answered Nan's inquiry. Yes, Hester Higgin lived there, she said. Hester was her daughter, but she was out at the moment. Could she take a message?

"Oh, yes, please!" said Nan eagerly. "Just tell her that Nan and Bert Bobbsey have a package belonging to her and that they will deliver it just as soon as possible. Yes, we have your address. Good-bye. There!" said Nan as she turned from the phone. "The address is 22 Cherry Road instead of Chester Road."

"I wish I'd known that before. It would have saved me a lot of trouble," said Bert.

In the kitchen they found Dinah seated at the table peeling vegetables for dinner.

"Where's the box?" Bert demanded.

"What box?" asked Dinah.

"We left one here on the table just a few minutes ago," replied Nan. "You must have seen it, Dinah."

"Lan' sakes, I don' see no box," said Dinah. "Less you mean de box Freddie and Flossie done took out into de garden," she added, brightening.

Nan and Bert looked at each other, then dashed outside the house. Their small brother and sister were not in sight, but a glance around showed that they had opened the box. The cover lay on the grass. The contents had spilled out, and the breeze was blowing them about. An envelope fluttered against Nan's foot, so she stooped to pick it up.

"Oh, look, Bert, it's a wedding invitation!" she cried. "There must have been dozens of them in that box. Now look at them! All over the garden!"

Nan began to pick up those heavy white envelopes which had been damaged.

"They are all ruined. Freddie and Flossie ought to pay for this," said Bert grimly. "I'll tell them a thing or two when I get hold of them."

"It's too bad," said Nan, worried. "I don't know how we are going to explain this to Miss Higgin."

The children had put back about half of the muddy, torn envelopes into the box when they saw a car drive up the street and stop before their house. A young, well-dressed woman got out of the auto and came up the walk. Nan and Bert heard her call out to someone, probably Flossie:

"Hello, little girl. Is this where Bert Bobbsey lives?"

CHAPTER II

THE WRONG TIME

FOR one awful moment it seemed to Nan Bobbsey as though her heart actually stopped beating. Then she gave a little gasp and looked at Bert.

"Do you suppose that can be Miss Higgin?" she whispered.

"We'll soon know," returned Bert. "Here she comes!"

Quick steps sounded on the driveway. A moment later Flossie appeared, closely followed by the young woman.

"There's my brother Bert," said Flossie. "And my sister Nan, too. They are twins, you know, just like Freddie and me."

The young lady smiled at Flossie. Then she came across the lawn toward Bert and held out her hand.

"I am Hester Higgin," she said. "I stopped at Mr. Jensen's, the engraver, for my wedding invitations. He told me he gave them to you to deliver.

Why, what's this?" she added, pausing in surprise to look at the open box. "Why, these look like—"

"They *are* your wedding invitations, Miss Higgin," said Bert. He shifted from one foot to the other. "Mr. Jensen did give them to me to deliver, but the address on the wrapping was wrong—and—"

Bert did not finish the sentence, for at that moment a gust of wind struck the open box and upset it. A second time the unfortunate envelopes were caught up by the breeze and blown all over the garden.

"Oh, stop them, catch them!" cried poor Miss Higgin. "Oh, oh, this is terrible!"

Freddie appeared at this moment, and with a shout began to rescue them.

"Don't worry. I'll get them!" he cried.

To those of our readers who are not already acquainted with the Bobbsey Twins, we will take a moment to explain that there are two sets: dark-haired Nan and Bert, the older pair, and Freddie and Flossie, the mischievous, golden-haired little twins.

The Bobbsey family live in Lakeport where Mr. Bobbsey is in the lumber business. They have two servants. Dinah is the cook, whom we have met already. Her husband, Sam Johnson, is the gardener and general handyman about the place.

Many adventures have befallen the little family. The latest one concerns their experiences in Radio Land, where they actually were in a play in a big broadcasting studio.

Now let us return to the children out in the garden and the mussed up wedding invitations. Just when Miss Higgin or one of the twins was about to pick up an envelope, along would come a gust of wind and pull it right from under their fingers!

To make matters worse, Waggo was attracted by the noise and excitement. He bounded out into the garden and joined in the chase. Waggo, as you will remember, was the Bobbseys' young dog.

He was a nice and very friendly little animal but he was only a puppy, and like all puppies, was full of mischief. He caught one of the envelopes in his mouth and gave a growl of joy. Then he began to chew it into a limp, pulpy mass.

Nan got the invitation away from him, but too late. She held it by a torn corner and looked sadly at Miss Higgin.

"I'm terribly sorry," she said. "I'm afraid your invitations are ruined. It's all our fault."

"We're getting 'em," panted Freddie, racing about the garden. "We have almost all of 'em now, haven't we, Flossie?"

"Except what Waggo's got," agreed Flossie. "He's lying on a couple."

Bert rolled Waggo over, took away the envelopes, and handed them to Miss Higgin. The young woman looked at them and tears filled her eyes.

"I don't know what to do," she murmured. "My wedding is close now. I am afraid I won't be able to have other invitations made in time. I am late with them as it is." She took the box Bert handed to her and turned away, tears in her eyes.

"Oh, please don't go," begged Nan. "Bert hasn't told you just what happened. Won't you please come into the house?" she added anxiously. "Dinah will make you a cup of tea. Perhaps we will think of something to do about the wedding invitations."

"Thank you. I think I will," said Miss Higgin. She put away her pocket handkerchief and looked at Bert. "I *am* a little curious to know what happened," she added.

Dinah had paid very little attention to what was going on in the garden. Now she looked with surprise at the five who filed through her kitchen.

"Yas'm," she said in answer to Nan's request for a cup of tea. "I'll fix up a tray in just a minute, Miss Nan. You-all cain't bring dat dog in here," she added sharply as Waggo was about to follow Freddie into the kitchen, "lessen you wipe off his feet. Dey's all full o' mud."

Freddie tied poor Waggo outside the house. Then carefully he wiped his own shoes before following his brother and sisters.

"Mr. Jensen put the wrong address on the box," Bert was saying as Freddie entered the living room. "I went there, found there wasn't any house at all, and brought the package home with me."

"Then we called up all the Higgins we could find in the telephone book," Nan added. She went on to tell how at last they had located Miss Higgin's mother.

"Bert was going to take the package right over to you. When we went to look for it on the kitchen table where we had left the box it was gone."

"We took it," Freddie interrupted eagerly. "Dinah told us not to open it in the house so we took it out into the garden."

"We thought there might be cookies in it," Flossie added.

"So when you found there weren't cookies you left the cover off the box. Then all Miss Higgin's nice wedding invitations blew about the garden and got spoiled," said Nan severely. "Wasn't that a naughty thing to do?"

"Y-yes, I guess so," said Freddie, looking very sorry indeed.

Miss Higgin took a sip of the tea Dinah had placed on a tray beside her, and broke off a piece of hot buttered toast. There was color in her cheeks and she looked very pretty, the twins thought. She seemed more cheerful, too. Catching the gaze of the little twins, she nodded and smiled at them.

"I like cookies too," she confided. "I really don't blame you very much for opening the box."

"But your ruined invitations!" Nan protested.

"It seems to me Mr. Jensen is more to blame than any one else," said Miss Higgin firmly. "He should have put the right address on the package in the first place. Then he should have seen to it that the box was delivered safely."

"Perhaps he could make some more in time," Bert suggested. "Anyway, I'm going to find out," and he went over to the telephone.

Nan tried to listen to Bert's conversation, but Freddie and Flossie were chattering at such a great rate with Miss Higgin that she could only make out a word here and there. As Bert crossed the room toward them the bride-to-be looked up expectantly.

"Well?" she questioned. "What did Mr. Jensen say? Can he make me some more?"

"I'm afraid not," said Bert. "He says it's too late now to get them ready in time for your wedding. I'm terribly sorry. Really I am!"

CHAPTER III

HELP NEEDED

MISS HIGGIN had half risen from her chair as Bert left the phone. Now she sank back again with a little sigh of disappointment.

"But I *must* have engraved invitations," she murmured. "I can't just phone to people and ask them to my wedding."

Nan had opened her mouth to speak when she heard the rattle of a key in the front door.

"I believe that's Daddy Bobbsey," she cried eagerly.

"It is!" shouted Freddie. Followed by Flossie, he flung himself upon his father as Mr. Bobbsey came in the front door. "Daddy, there's a pretty lady here and we spoiled all her env'lopes so she can't have any wedding."

"We thought they were cookies!" added Flossie helpfully.

"Well, that makes it all as clear as day," laughed Mr. Bobbsey.

15

He hoisted Freddie up to one shoulder, kissed Flossie and raised her to his other shoulder. In this manner he entered the living room. He smiled at Nan, Bert and Miss Higgin, to whom Nan hastened to present her father.

"What is all this I hear about envelopes and weddings and cookies?" he asked. "I must admit I'm all at sea."

The twins looked at their father with eyes full of love. They were positive that Daddy Bobbsey was the most perfect parent in the world. They believed that he could solve all their problems for them, whether they be great or small.

Now he listened attentively while Nan and Bert told him the story of the ruined wedding invitations.

"We never should have left the box on the kitchen table. Of course, Freddie and Flossie should not have opened it," Bert stated. "But it's too late to think of that now."

"You can get some more env'lopes, can't you, Daddy?" asked Flossie, nestling up to her father.

"I don't know, Fat Fairy," said Mr. Bobbsey, stroking the little girl's curls. He looked across at Miss Higgin. She had finished her tea and had placed her napkin on the tray beside her.

"I don't need to tell you how sorry I am all this has happened," Mr. Bobbsey said. "Of course, I hold myself responsible for the damage to your invitations and will see to it that you receive others just as soon as it is possible to have them engraved."

"I'm afraid therein lies the difficulty," said Miss Higgin. "There won't be time to have more made before the wedding."

"Did Mr. Jensen say that?"

Nan nodded. "Bert just phoned him," she said.

"Um! Well, that does upset matters." Mr. Bobbsey pushed Flossie away gently, got up and walked over to the window. The twins watched him anxiously, wondering if he would be able to find a way out of the trouble.

"I have it!" he cried suddenly, turning around. "I think I know the man who will do it for us."

"An engraver?" asked Miss Higgin eagerly.

"Yes, and a good friend of mine," said Mr. Bobbsey. "I'll call him up at once. Are you free to go down to his place now," he asked of Miss Higgin, "if I can make an appointment?"

"Oh, yes, the sooner the better! I'll be so grateful if you can fix this up for me," said the young woman.

Mr. Bobbsey nodded and called the number. After a few moments of conversation with his friend he put down the receiver, looking very well pleased.

"Well, you heard me make the appointment," he said, smiling at them. "Now come along and let's see what we can do. All ready?"

"Oh, may we go?" cried Flossie, clapping her hands. "All of us?"

"If Miss Higgin doesn't mind," smiled Mr. Bobbsey. "The car is right outside and there's plenty of room in it for us all."

Miss Higgin and Flossie got in the front seat beside Daddy Bobbsey. Freddie, Nan and Bert rode in the back.

They were just starting off when there came a wild barking from the garden. Waggo dashed around the side of the house trailing a length of rope.

"I tied him up but he must have got loose. May we take him with us, Daddy?" begged Freddie.

"All right, but hurry," agreed Mr. Bobbsey.

Freddie opened the door. Waggo jumped head first to the seat beside the little boy. He sat there as happy as could be, with his tongue hanging out and his mouth stretched in a canine grin. Waggo liked to ride almost as much as Freddie and Flossie did.

A short drive brought them to the heart of the Lakeport business section. Mr. Bobbsey turned into a side street and stopped before a shop which bore a sign: SAMUEL HARTWIG, EN-GRAVER.

"Well, here we are," said Mr. Bobbsey, reaching across Miss Higgin to open the door for her.

All but Freddie went into the store. He had to stay in the car and keep Waggo company. Mr. Hartwig came from an inner room to greet the party and seemed very glad to see Mr. Bobbsey. He shook hands with Nan and Bert, patted Flossie on the head and bowed politely to Miss Higgin. When Mr. Bobbsey told him what they wanted he shook his head.

"That is only a very little time you give me," he said, speaking with a foreign accent. "An engraver's work, as you know, Mr. Bobbsey, is an art. It cannot be too much hurried. I would do most anything for a valued friend but this time I am afraid I cannot oblige."

"If all your other work were set aside say for just a few days, could you do it?" asked Daddy Bobbsey.

Nan and Bert and little Flossie regarded Mr. Hartwig anxiously. Miss Higgin fairly held her breath while she waited for his answer.

"Well, of course," he said, "it might be possible—"

"Good!" cried the children's father quickly. "Then you will do it?"

The engraver glanced from Mr. Bobbsey to Miss Higgin. He took off his glasses and polished them very carefully. Then he returned them to his nose. He shook his head and sighed.

"It is a very foolish thing," he said slowly. "I should make no such promise. But I am a foolish old man and—I will do it!"

Nan and Bert beamed happily. Flossie clapped her hands and jumped up and down. Hester Higgin reached across the counter to take Mr. Hartwig's hand in her own.

"Thank you so much," she said.

"Believe me, I will never forget this, Hartwig," said Daddy Bobbsey warmly. "Maybe I can do you a favor some time."

Miss Higgin left one of the soiled, crumpled invitations as a sample of what she would like. She thanked Mr. Hartwig again for his kindness and went out of the shop with Mr. Bobbsey and the twins.

"And now, if you will give me your address," said Mr. Bobbsey as he opened the car door, "I will drive you home, Miss Higgin."

"She lives at 22 Cherry Road," Bert stated.

"That's right," laughed Nan. She thought of all the phoning she and Bert had done earlier in the day.

When they reached 22 Cherry Road Miss Higgin insisted that the Bobbseys come in with her for a few minutes.

"I want you to meet my mother and father," she said, adding with a grateful smile, "I'm sure they will want to thank you for all the trouble you have taken over my wedding invitations."

The Higgins lived in an old-fashioned house set well back from the street. Shrubs and trees dotted the lawn and beautiful flowers made the place very pretty.

Mrs. Higgin herself met the callers at the front door and invited them into the living room. A man of middle age, who rose to greet them, looked so much like Miss Higgin that the twins and Mr. Bobbsey knew he must be her father.

The Bobbseys liked these people at once. Mr. and Mrs. Higgin were much interested in the story of the wedding invitations. They were more grateful to Daddy Bobbsey than he felt he deserved for the part he had played in straightening the matter out.

From the subject of wedding invitations the conversation naturally turned to the wedding. The Bobbseys learned from Mrs. Higgin that the ceremony was to be held at a quaint Dutch settlement near the Higgins' summer home.

"The place is called Tuliptown," Mrs. Higgin explained.

"You have some pictures of it, haven't you,

Mother?" asked Mr. Higgin. "Maybe the children would like to see them."

"The pictures show many scenes in Tuliptown," said the lady. "Some are of Windmill Cottage. That's a nice boarding house run by Mrs. Van Doorn. She is a lovely person and cooks the most delicious meals you can imagine."

"Is there a windmill in the cottage?" Freddie asked.

"Bless you, no!" laughed Mrs. Higgin. "There is one on the grounds, though," she added. "A windmill so old and rickety that people say it is unsafe and should be pulled down."

The twins liked the pictures of the Dutch settlement. They thought Windmill Cottage looked very quaint and pretty in its setting of tall trees. What interested them most, however, were the pictures of windmills. Especially interesting to them was the dark, decrepit-looking one on the cottage grounds.

"I'd like to go to that place," said Nan, her eyes shining. "It's so different from anything I've ever seen."

"Well, why don't you come down during your summer vacation?" Mrs. Higgin suggested hospitably. "I'm sure Mrs. Van Doorn would be glad to have you."

"Oh, Daddy, could we?" cried Nan eagerly.

"Well, well, we'll see," said Mr. Bobbsey.

"That means we can go," said Flossie, clapping her hands.

"Whoa, not so fast, young lady," laughed her daddy. "I haven't said so yet."

Everybody smiled at the face Flossie made. Then Mr. Bobbsey rose and said they really must be starting for home as it was growing late.

Just before they left, Miss Higgin made a surprising and thrilling suggestion. She invited the Bobbseys to her wedding and then asked the younger twins to be a part of her bridal party!

CHAPTER IV

GREAT PLANS

ALL the way home the children talked about this unexpected invitation to take part in Miss Higgin's wedding. Bert and Freddie were interested chiefly because the event would give them a chance to see Tuliptown and its fascinating windmills.

Nan and Flossie, however, had all a girl's interest in the wedding itself. Almost before they had left the Higgins' house they had begun to make plans about what they would wear and the kind of wedding presents they would give.

Of course, all this was new to Mrs. Bobbsey and had to be gone over and over from beginning to end for her benefit after they reached home. Since most of the story was told at the table, little attention was paid to Dinah's excellent dinner that night. It was necessary to remind the twins again and again to eat their steak and potatoes, while in their minds they could see only windmills and rows of Dutch cottages!

"You make it sound very attractive, I must say," said Mrs. Bobbsey at last. "I like what you tell me about Tuliptown and Windmill Cottage and the Higgin family, too."

"I'm glad you do," said Nan hopefully.

"Then may we take part in the wedding?" begged Flossie.

"And stay at Windmill Cottage afterward?" added Freddie.

Mrs. Bobbsey glanced at Daddy Bobbsey, who nodded and smiled.

"Why not?" he said.

"All right, we will!" said Mrs. Bobbsey with a gay laugh. "First the Higgin wedding, then to Windmill Cottage for a nice long vacation."

"Hooray!" cried Freddie, jumping up to hug his mother. "Golly, won't we have fun! And I'm going to ride on the windmill, too," he added.

"You can't ride on a windmill," Bert protested.

"Yes, I can. On the part that goes round and looks like a Ferris wheel," explained Freddie.

"You'd soon find out the difference if you were to try it," Bert said.

Mr. Bobbsey added, "Riding on a windmill is out of the question, Freddie. If we let you go to Tuliptown you must try to behave and not get into trouble. Promise?"

Freddie promised, but he was disappointed just

the same. He had counted on riding the windmill wheel.

The next few days were very busy ones for the Bobbsey Twins. School was almost out. They were very thankful for this, as there were a great many things they had to do before Miss Higgin's wedding.

Freddie had been chosen to carry the wedding ring. The thought of this weighed heavily on the little fellow's mind. One day he said to Nan:

"Have you an old ring I could play with?"

"Why yes, I guess so," replied his sister. "What do you want to do with it?"

"Practise for the wedding," announced the little boy. "Do you suppose you could help me, and Bert too? Maybe Flossie ought to practise what she has to do. What does she have to do, anyway?"

"Carry a basket of flowers and scatter them in the aisle of the church before the bride walks in," explained Nan. "I think your idea about practising is a good one. Get Bert and Flossie. I'll look for a ring and a basket."

Bert had gone to Charlie Mason's house, so Nan had to help the younger twins alone. First they tried to find some music on the radio by which they could walk in time. It seemed as if Freddie hardly had a chance to get the ring balanced on a pillow and to start his march before the piece would stop.

"Maybe Dinah will sing for us," giggled Flossie.

"She sings only hymns," objected Freddie. "She doesn't know wedding marches."

"Let's ask her," said Nan, and called to the cook.

Dinah came into the living room and when she heard what the children wanted of her, she laughed so hard she shook all over.

"Lawsee, poor ole Dinah ain't done no singin' fo' so long, Ah declares Ah done forgot how. But Ah'll try, just to help a good cause—dat is, if Ah can be sure dat husband ob mine Sam don't hear me!"

"He drove Mother downtown," said Nan, "so you have nothing to worry about."

Dinah in a loud, deep voice started to sing the well-known tune of the wedding march, but the words she put in it were only dum-dum-de-dum over and over again. Freddie and Flossie were solemn as they practised, but Nan had to bite her lips to keep from laughing aloud.

"How are we doing?" asked Freddie, who was really very proud of himself.

"Does it look nice," asked Flossie, "when I throw these flowers? Course they are only make-believe ones. Miss Higgin said I'd have real ones at the wedding."

"Everything looks very nice," said Nan. "Do it once more and then we had better stop. Poor Dinah won't have any breath left!"

In the middle of the next march the swinging door to the dining room was thrown open suddenly and in rushed Waggo. Straight for the wedding party he went. First he jumped on Flossie and knocked the basket of flowers from her hand. Then he pounced on Freddie, who dropped the ring. Away it rolled out of sight under the sofa.

"You bad dog," cried Flossie, "you haven't any manners at all."

"Dat dog'll drive old Dinah crazy," said the cook. "You git out o' here!" she added, chasing Waggo ahead of her into the kitchen.

It took poor Freddie a long time to find the ring, and later he had more bad luck in losing it several times. It seemed to disappear easily and had to be hunted almost every day.

Of course, there was the important matter of wedding presents to be considered. Neither Nan nor Bert had a great deal of money to spend, so they wisely decided to make their gifts for the bride, instead of buying them.

"People always like things that are made for them anyway," Nan said, "even if the presents don't cost much."

"I believe I could build a weather vane," said

Bert thoughtfully. "We had to do that in shop class this term and I think I remember how."

"Oh Bert, that would be nice! Do you think you could make it in the shape of a windmill?"

Bert looked as if he were not sure. However, the thought evidently appealed to him for after a moment he said:

"I've never tried anything like that, but I might be able to do it. It's a good idea, anyway."

For her present to Miss Higgin Nan decided to make a pretty apron of some light material and then to embroider a little windmill in one corner of it. She told Flossie about it one Saturday morning as Mrs. Bobbsey was getting ready to drive the girls downtown to do some shopping.

"I think I'll get the material this morning," Nan decided. "If I have any left over I'll make a dress for your doll."

"Then I hope you have some left over," said Flossie. "Did you know Mother's going to let me pick out my own dress for the wedding?"

Mrs. Bobbsey appeared just then and whisked her two daughters away. They stopped first at Daddy Bobbsey's office to make an appointment with him for luncheon, then went on to a department store.

After Nan had bought some dainty dotted swiss for the apron, they went to the pattern counter.

With a little bounce of excitement Flossie jumped up on a high stool and began to turn the pages of the pattern book.

"Mother, may I have anything I want?" she asked. "Really and truly?"

"Really and truly," returned Mrs. Bobbsey, smiling. "That is, if you will pick something suitable for a very little girl," she added cautiously.

"Oh, I will," said Flossie.

At last she found just what she wished. She stood up on the rungs of her chair and brought her hand down with a soft little plop on the book.

"Look, Mother! This is the prettiest one of—"

With that Flossie lost her balance. The stool and the little girl fell to the floor with a great thud. People turned around and the saleswoman hurried from behind the counter.

Flossie insisted she was not hurt. She was brushed off and then the pattern was bought.

"I'm hungry," said Nan as they turned away from the counter. "Isn't it time to meet Daddy?"

Mrs. Bobbsey looked at her wrist watch and nodded.

"Just about," she said. "I imagine he may be waiting for us now in the lobby of the hotel."

At the same time that Mrs. Bobbsey and the girls were going to meet Daddy Bobbsey, Freddie was coming from a hardware store where he had been sent by Bert to purchase a can of green paint. He held the tin under his arm and started off at a quick pace.

He knew Dinah was making fish chowder for he had smelled it as he was starting out on his errand. Now it was nearly lunch time and Freddie had the healthy appetite of all small boys. The delightful odor seemed to beckon him on. He hastened his steps until soon he was running along.

As he turned a corner Freddie nearly bumped into a group of older boys. Still thinking only of Dinah's fish chowder, Freddie tried to hurry past them. One of the boys put out an arm and stopped the young Bobbsey twin.

"What's your rush, little boy?" he asked teasingly. "Where's the fire?"

Freddie felt his face grow red. He hated to be called a little boy, perhaps because he *was* a little boy, and couldn't do much about it.

"There isn't any fire," he said soberly. "I was just going home."

The boys laughed as though this were a great joke. The one who had stopped him reached down and grabbed the paint can from under his arm.

"What's this? Your lunch?" he jeered. "Maybe it's a can of soup, fellows. Here, catch!"

Freddie stamped his foot and tears of helpless fury stung his eyes.

"You give me that!" he cried. "It belongs to me and you give it to me!"

"Says who!" jeered his tormentor, tossing the can a little higher in the air. "Do you hear that, fellows? Shall we give it back to him?"

"No," they laughed, taking their cue from the leader. One of them stepped into the road and held up his hands. "Here, give us a real toss," he invited.

While the can of paint was in the air, a heavy truck lumbered around the corner. The boy dodged to avoid the big machine and failed to catch the tin which fell in the street. One of the wheels went over it, leaving a crushed and shapeless mass from which green paint oozed stickily.

CHAPTER V

GETTING EVEN

HOLDING back the tears with an effort, Freddie went out into the road to save what he could of the green paint. He picked up the shapeless mass of tin and found that it was almost empty. There was not enough left in it to take any home.

The little boy swallowed the lump in his throat and looked about him. Satisfied that the bullies had disappeared, he drew his arm hastily across his eyes to wipe away the tears and started on.

When Freddie reached the house he went around the back to the kitchen. The first thing he smelled when he opened the kitchen door was Dinah's fish chowder, but somehow the little boy no longer felt hungry.

He was wondering how he could tell Bert about the can of paint. He knew his brother was in a hurry for it and that he had spent the last cent of his weekly allowance to pay for it. Freddie wondered if there was enough in his own little china pig bank to buy some more.

"Dinah, do you know where Bert is?" he asked.

"He's still in the garage, honey, fussin' wid dat windmill he's makin'," returned the cook, busily stirring something in a large pot. "You tell him to come get his lunch. Hurry up an' get yo'self washed, chile. I 'spect you must be starved."

"I'll be back in just a minute," Freddie promised. "I have to see Bert first."

The small boy went very slowly across the grass to the garage. The door was open, so he could hear Bert whistling a merry tune while he worked. Freddie's feet dragged as he walked.

"Hello," his brother greeted, poking his head out. "Come along with that can of paint. I'm all ready for it."

Freddie swallowed and scuffed the toe of his small shoe against the sidewalk.

"I—haven't got it," he confessed.

"What? You haven't gone yet?" In his surprise Bert came out of the garage, the half finished weather vane in his hand. "Hey, what is this? I sent you for that paint a half hour ago."

"I did buy it," said Freddie. He gulped, then went on miserably, "When I was coming home some big boys took the can away from me. They played ball with it."

"Oh, they did, did they!" said Bert. "Well, I hope they had a good time."

"Yes, I guess they did," said poor Freddie. "One of them threw it and it dropped in the road. A truck ran over it. I couldn't do anything about it," he pleaded. "They were big boys and there were a lot of them."

"You couldn't do anything, but *I* can," said Bert angrily. "Do you know who these boys are?" he added.

Freddie replied that he did not know their names, though he had seen them before. He described them so well that Bert knew at once who they were.

"It's Buddy Brower and his crowd," he said. "They think they're smart, going around pulling girls' hair and picking on little kids."

"What are you going to do?" demanded Freddie as Bert put the weather vane back in the garage and picked up his sweater.

"I'm going to find Buddy Brower and make him pay for my green paint."

"Maybe you better do that later," Freddie suggested. "Dinah says the fish chowder is all ready. She wants us both to come in to lunch."

Even Bert's anger at Buddy Brower was not strong enough to overcome the thought of Dinah's meal. He decided to eat first and find the bully afterward.

"Coming?" he asked Freddie half an hour later

when he was ready to find the bully. "Like to see how Buddy Brower looks when somebody picks on *him*?"

The younger twin's eyes sparkled. "Yes, I would," he agreed, adding sturdily, "Maybe I can help you."

A few minutes' walk brought the two boys to the part of town where Freddie had met with trouble. Sure enough, there was a big smear of green paint in the middle of the road. The crushed tin can, looking even more battered than when the little fellow had last seen it, lay limp against the gutter.

Of course, there was no sign of Buddy Brower and his crowd of bullies but Bert said he thought he knew where to find them.

A few blocks farther on was an open lot. As the boys neared this place they could hear shouts and sounds of quarreling. A ball game was in progress.

"This is where Buddy Brower usually plays," said Bert.

Freddie drew back a little fearfully. After all, there were several in the crowd, while he and Bert were all alone. The little boy knew that his brother was very brave and not afraid of anyone, especially when he was angry. Suppose, though, they all should attack him?

As it happened, Freddie need not have worried. All bullies are cowards as everyone knows. When one of the crowd saw Bert coming and realized who he was, and that he probably was bound to get revenge, he yelled, "Better beat it, fellows. Here comes trouble!" Then he made off as fast as he could for the opposite side of the street.

The others followed his example. However, the one who was standing close to Bert and Freddie, and who happened to be Buddy Brower himself, was not quick enough. He started to run, but Freddie darted across the boy's path and gripped him by the leg.

Down went Buddy flat on his back and down went Freddie with him, still clinging to the leg! The bully aimed a blow at the little boy's head. Before his hand could descend, Bert had gripped it roughly.

"Let go, Freddie!" he commanded. Seizing Buddy by an arm and the collar of his jacket, he dragged him to his feet. "Now then," said Bert, "do you want to fight?"

Buddy hesitated, glared at the Bobbsey boy and looked about him at the deserted field. Seeing that his friends had left him and that his challenger was not only a boy of his own size but one who was evidently looking for a fight, Buddy lost the swaggering manner he had shown before.

"What do you want?" he demanded sharply. "What's the idea of picking a scrap with a guy? What have I done to you?"

"You know well enough what you've done," said Bert. "And you know what I want, too."

"You're crazy," blustered the Brower boy. "I don't know what you're talking about."

"I'm thinking of a can of green paint." Bert walked a threatening step closer to the bully. "The one you took from my little brother and played ball with. The one that got run over by the truck."

"Yeah? Well, what about it?" growled the boy.

"You are going to buy me a new can," said Bert.

Buddy hesitated, but as Bert took another threatening step toward him he thrust his hand hastily into his pocket.

"How much?" he wanted to know.

Bert mentioned the price and Buddy counted some coins in his hand and gave them to the Bobbsey boy.

"That's right. Next time you want a little fun," said Bert as a parting shot, "you'd better pick on a fellow your own size."

As he and Freddie left the bully and turned

toward the paint store, Bert smiled at his little brother.

"That wasn't a bad flying tackle you made, Freddie," he said. "I couldn't have done better myself."

The little boy beamed. "I'm going to play football some day," he announced sturdily. "On my college team."

During the week following the incident of the green paint the Bobbsey Twins learned of the arrival in a neighboring town of Hans Weser's carnival. From all reports it was a very good one, with many amusement booths, a merry-go-round, a Ferris wheel, and numerous other attractions. Daddy Bobbsey said he would drive the family over there on Saturday.

The day seemed a long time in coming but at last it arrived. Directly after luncheon the family set off for the carnival.

When they reached the show grounds the place was crowded. The twins kept close to their parents, and looked about them with eager eyes. Freddie clutched his beloved fire engine against his chest. He had insisted upon bringing it with him in the hope, as he had told his family, there would be a fire and he would be called upon to help put it out.

Beside the many other attractions the carnival

boasted a small zoo. The children made the rounds of the cages, looking curiously at a zebra, an emu, and a group of African monkeys.

Nan meanwhile had stopped at a booth which attracted her by its unusual decorations. A row of small dolls dressed in Dutch costumes lined the back, while in the foreground were cartons of tempting homemade candy. The boxes themselves were made in the form of Dutch houses. The peaked roofs, which folded back, were the covers.

"How pretty!" cried Nan. "I must have one of them!"

The girl in charge of the booth smiled at Nan. She was beautiful. Her blond hair, blue eyes and rosy cheeks were set off by the Dutch costume she wore. Nan chose one of the little candy houses, and as it was being wrapped she said impulsively:

"I am interested in anything that looks Dutch just now. I am going to spend my vacation at Windmill Cottage near a little Dutch settlement called Tuliptown."

"Why, I come from Tuliptown," smiled the pretty girl. "My name is Juliana so you see I really belong in a Dutch settlement."

Before Nan could comment on this interesting fact, she felt a touch on her shoulder and found Mrs. Bobbsey beside her.

"Oh, Mother," she cried, "this young lady's

name is Juliana and she comes from Tuliptown. Isn't that interesting?"

"I have some tulips for sale, or I should say tulip bulbs," said the pretty girl, smiling at Mrs. Bobbsey. "If planted this fall, they will give you a garden full of lovely blooms in the spring."

"I know the Dutch people are famous for their tulips," said Mrs. Bobbsey. "I'll take a dozen bulbs in assorted colors."

While she and Nan were making their purchases and talking to the pretty girl about Tuliptown, Freddie and Flossie discovered the Ferris wheel. The device had been built to look like a windmill. The most wonderful part about it was that it was operated by several dwarfs dressed in leather jerkins and breeches and peaked caps.

"They look like the gnomes in my book of fairy stories," whispered Flossie.

"Oh, Daddy, may we have a ride on the windmill?" begged Freddie.

Mr. Bobbsey consented. Since it was a very small one he permitted the children to ride on it alone.

"While you are having your fun I am going to look for Bert," he said. "But you stay right here. Don't go away until I come back," he charged them.

Freddie and Flossie had more than one turn

on the Ferris wheel; in fact, they had three. When their money was all gone, and Daddy Bobbsey had not yet returned, they began to look about them for fresh amusement.

Freddie thought of a story his mother had once read to him in which a deserving little boy had found a treasure hidden in the base of a windmill. He thought it might be fun to explore this one, in the hope of finding a treasure all by himself

He and Flossie went around to the back where no one could see them; secrecy, as Freddie well knew, was a very important part of a treasure hunt! He looked for an opening large enough for them to crawl through.

They found one, but it was rather small and very close to the ground. Flossie eyed it doubtfully and drew back, but Freddie told her to go on.

"Go ahead," her twin urged. "I'll come after you when I have killed the dragon like in the story."

Flossie got her head and shoulders through the opening but came up against a solid block of wood which housed the machinery of the Ferris wheel. She tried to draw back, but found to her amazement and sudden terror that she could not do so. She was hopelessly stuck in the opening of the mill!

CHAPTER VI

AT THE CARNIVAL

BERT had become separated from the rest of the family when his attention had been attracted to a circus ring. In it a group of spirited horses were being put through their paces.

The Bobbsey boy had always liked horses, so now he paused to watch the beautiful animals. As he stood there a jolly looking man walked up to him and started talking.

"Admire horses, do you?" he asked.

"You bet I do," the lad returned eagerly. "I'd like to live on a farm where I could ride all I want to."

"You don't find horses like these on farms," said the man with a hearty laugh. He put his hand on the bridle of a beautiful black stallion with a starred forehead and drew him forward. "How would you like to ride this fellow?" he asked.

"I'd like it," said Bert eagerly. "Say, wouldn't

it be great to own a horse like that! He's a beauty."

"How about taking him for a little canter?" the man suggested. "It will cost you only a quarter for a five-minute ride."

Bert willingly paid the fee. The man held the horse for him as he vaulted into the saddle. The animal shied and danced a few steps toward one of the booths. Bert tightened his grip on the reins, said "Gid-dap there!" and clapped his heels against the horse's ribs. The animal responded, and off they went into a cleared space in the crowd, Bert holding tightly to the reins.

It was great fun seeing the people and the various amusements of the carnival from a place so high up. Bert was attempting to pick out his own little family group, when there came a sudden loud outcry from the direction of the windmill Ferris wheel.

The boy saw people stare in that direction and could feel the surge of the crowd against his horse. The beast shied nervously and wheeled about. Bert tried to check the animal, but was too late. He heard a crash and a shout of dismay. Looking down, he saw that his horse had backed into the stand of a peanut vendor, upsetting it and scattering the nuts all over the ground.

To make matters even worse, Bert's mount

chose that moment to take the bit in his teeth and bolt! People scattered to left and right before him. Bert looked into startled faces, saw mouths agape and heard terrified screams and shouts.

Suddenly a man darted from the crowd and flung himself at the horse's head. He caught the bridle and hung on. For a hundred feet or so he half ran and was half dragged along in danger of being trampled by the frightened animal.

After a moment, the furious pace slackened, the horse slowed to a walk, then came to a sudden quivering stop. The man took his hand from the bridle, patted the animal soothingly, and grinned up at Bert.

"I guess you can get down now, son," he said. "Figure you've had enough riding for one day. Am I right?"

Bert nodded and slipped to the ground. He held out his hand to his rescuer.

"I'm certainly much obliged to you, sir," he said. "I guess you kept a lot of people in the crowd from getting hurt."

Bert's new acquaintance started to reply, when suddenly his gaze became fixed. The lad followed his glance and saw that a crowd had gathered around the windmill Ferris wheel. He noticed something else, too. The peanut vendor's stand was on fire!

The Bobbsey boy returned the now gentle horse to its owner, then darted to the aid of the peanut vendor. He picked up an old sack near by and began beating out the flames.

Meanwhile, what was happening to poor little Flossie, stuck in the base of the Ferris wheel? Her cries and Freddie's shouts for help had brought several people hurrying to the scene; in fact, it had been that excitement which had made all the trouble for Bert.

Daddy Bobbsey was one of the first to reach the place. He saw Flossie with her head and shoulders wedged in the hole at the base of the windmill and for a moment did not know whether to laugh or to scold the little girl. He ended by doing neither, for when he came a little closer he saw that his "fat fairy" was genuinely frightened. He knelt down and put an arm about her.

"It's Daddy, dear," he said soothingly. "There's nothing to be afraid of. Do just as I tell you and I'll have you out of here in a few minutes."

Flossie's sobs subsided. She gave one shuddering sigh, then stood very still.

"Y-yes, Daddy," she said in a small voice.

"First put your arms straight above your head and as far in front of your face as you can," Mr. Bobbsey instructed. "Better clasp your hands. Now—ready?"

"Y-yes," said Flossie.

Very gently Mr. Bobbsey began to pull his little girl free from her prison. The crowd looked on with sympathy, now and then offering a word of advice.

At last Flossie's shoulders were free. Then her tousled little head and flushed, tear-stained face came into view. She flung her arms about her daddy and clung to him, hiding her face against his shoulder.

Holding her tightly, Mr. Bobbsey got to his feet. The crowd, seeing that the excitement was over, had started to leave. Now the little girl's father began to look about for her twin, but could not find him.

"Where is the young rascal!" he exclaimed, beginning to lose patience. "He was here just a minute ago. Freddie!" he called. "Freddie, where are you!"

There was no answer, for the little boy, his precious fire engine clasped in his arms, was rushing across the carnival grounds toward the peanut vendor's stand. Freddie had seen smoke, and knew that where there is smoke there usually is fire. Where there is a fire there are generally fire engines. Had not Freddie brought his fire engine to the carnival for just such an emergency?

Unfortunately, the carnival grounds were very

wide and Freddie's legs were rather short. He ran as fast as he could but he was very much afraid that the blaze would be put out before he could get there.

In and out among a sea of legs dodged Freddie, clinging to his precious toy. The flames were very near now; he could see the curling smoke right ahead of him.

Suddenly something tripped him. Before he could recover himself, poor Freddie had plunged headlong into a heap of burned peanuts!

CHAPTER VII

MISCHIEF

LUCKILY for Freddie, the fire was out. Even so, the burned mess about the vendor's stand was uncomfortably hot and somewhat sooty. The little boy picked himself up and rubbed a hand across his face, leaving a long, black smear.

"You're a sight," said Bert, regarding his small brother critically. "Why can't you look where you're going?"

"I wanted to help put out the fire," Freddie explained.

"We'll have to get you washed off," said Bert. "Oh, hello, Dad," he called as Mr. Bobbsey came up with Flossie.

His father, usually so good-natured, was looking distinctly annoyed with his small family. He set Flossie on her feet and frowned at Freddie.

"Do you think you can keep out of mischief for five minutes if you try very hard?" he asked his small son.

Freddie looked at the ground and his chin quivered. "I—I only wanted to help put out the fire," he said.

Mr. Bobbsey looked at the wreck of the peanut stand.

"What's been happening here?" he wanted to know.

"He ride da horse. He backa up, knocka my stand in da dirt," said the peanut vendor, pointing accusingly at Bert. "Stand catcha fire. Now all my peanuts, she ruined."

"So that's the way it is," said Mr. Bobbsey with a grim glance at Bert. "Well, never mind, Tony, my good fellow. I'll pay for the damage to your stand, whatever it is. Here," he reached in his pocket for some money which he handed to the Italian, "will that make things all right with you?"

Instantly the vendor was all smiles. He accepted the bills with many thanks. Then Mr. Bobbsey breathed more easily. His troubles were not yet at an end, however. Just as he was about to gather up his children and go in search of Mrs. Bobbsey and Nan, a fat-faced, important acting little man elbowed his way through the crowd and barred their path.

"You Mr. Bobbsey?" asked this person.

"Yes," said Daddy Bobbsey, adding politely, "What can I do for you?"

The stranger leveled his finger at Bert and the little twins. They saw with surprise that he was trembling with rage.

"The only thing you can do for me," said the fat-faced man, "is to take your children away from my carnival and keep them away. They are mischievous and make trouble for me. I do not want them here!"

"Well, and may I ask who you are?" asked Mr. Bobbsey quietly.

"I am Hans Weser of Tuliptown," said the little man, drawing himself up to his full height, which was not very great and thrusting out his chest. "I had a little trouble there, so I took my carnival away from that town. Now I come here and I have more trouble, all on account of your children."

"You may set your mind at rest," said Daddy Bobbsey shortly. "We are leaving and we won't be back, you may be sure of that."

"That is good," said the little man unpleasantly. "I am much pleased. Good day to you, sir!"

Bert and the little twins knew that their daddy was very much annoyed. He walked with his shoulders thrown back and his mouth pressed into a thin, straight line. The boy was the first to break the silence.

"I'm sorry I made trouble for you, Dad," he

said. "I guess I shouldn't have taken the ride on the horse without speaking to you and Mother first."

"And I shouldn't have dared Flossie to go into the mill," said Freddie.

"And I shouldn't have got my head stuck," added Flossie.

Daddy Bobsey smiled a little, and said that as long as they were sorry for the trouble they had caused it would be best to forget all about the naughty things they had done.

"I see Mother and Nan over there near the refreshment booth," he added. "How about buying some sandwiches and a bottle or two of soda?"

"Maybe we could go up to the lake and have a picnic," suggested Flossie.

"Good idea, my Fat Fairy," said her father, smiling at her. "If Mother says so, we'll do it."

Both Mrs. Bobbsey and Nan thought the suggestion a very good one. So, after arming themselves with sandwiches and lemonade they set out for further fun.

The lake was not far from the carnival grounds; in fact, Hans Weser had chosen his fair site so it could be near the water. The shore front offered many pretty spots for picnickers. It had also rowboats which the man was renting by the hour.

The Bobbseys found a place close to a water-fall and settled down under the shade of the trees to enjoy sandwiches and cooling drinks. While they ate, Mrs. Bobbsey and Nan told of meeting Miss Juliana, the pretty girl who had sold them candy and tulip bulbs and who came from Tulip-town.

"That's funny! The owner of the carnival comes from Tuliptown too," Bert commented. "His name is Hans Weser and he's a Dutchman."

After hearing more about him, Mrs. Bobbsey and Nan decided that they did not like Hans Weser very well. This feeling, you may be sure, was heartily shared by the rest of the Bobbsey family!

After they had finished eating the sandwiches down to the last crumb and had helped themselves to as much of Nan's box of homemade candy as their mother would permit, they decided to go rowing on the lake.

Daddy Bobbsey wondered if they should hire one of Hans Weser's boats. When the children promised to be very good and not get into any more mischief, he consented to take them with him.

The family drifted gently downstream. At one point where the lake widened they caught a glimpse of a farmhouse and a windmill.

"It isn't a very pretty windmill," said Flossie. "I like the wooden ones better."

"I should think you'd have had enough of them for one day," her Daddy teased.

Flossie looked thoughtful and said rather soberly, "Yes, I guess I have."

As they reached a bend in the stream another rowboat appeared, cutting directly across their path. Mr. Bobbsey, who was at the oars, stopped quickly to avoid it. As he did so, he recognized the young woman in the other boat as Hester Higgin. With her was a man. A moment later she showed by a smile and a wave of the hand that she remembered them also.

As the two boats drifted alongside, Miss Higgin introduced the person with her as Jack Benson, whom she was going to marry. He was a handsome, frank-spoken young man. He seemed genuinely glad to meet the twins, explaining that Hester had spoken of them and of the part they were to take in the Tuliptown wedding.

The mention of Tuliptown recalled to Nan's mind the girl in the Dutch booth. She described her, but before she could finish, Miss Higgin broke in delightedly.

"Juliana? Why, I guess I do know her!" she exclaimed. "She's my cousin. But I can't imagine," she added thoughtfully, "why she is here!"

"Oh, do you know him, too?" asked Bert in surprise.

"Of course I do," said Miss Higgin, adding scornfully, "I don't hear much good of him, either, I can tell you that." She glanced at her fiancé as if for confirmation and he nodded soberly.

"Hans Weser is a trouble-maker," he explained. "One of those people who likes to run the world, you know, and raises a big fuss when things don't go his way."

"Besides, he has queer ideas," Miss Higgin added. "He caused a great deal of unpleasantness in the little Dutch settlement and I imagine the people of Tuliptown are very glad to be rid of him."

"Mother, what's the matter?" asked Nan suddenly. "What are you looking at so strangely?"

"Your shoes. They are all wet," said Mrs. Bobbsey, worried. "I am very much afraid there is a leak in this boat!"

CHAPTER VIII

MORE TROUBLE

A LEAK in the boat!

Mrs. Bobbsey had said the words so quietly that for a moment the twins had not been alarmed. Now, however, they looked down at their feet and saw a film of water which grew and deepened as they watched.

Bert said suddenly, "I'll say there's a leak! It's right here under me. The water's coming in fast!"

Daddy Bobbsey glanced anxiously at the shore. The boat, heavily laden as it was, could not reach there in safety, he was sure.

"You can never make it," said Jack Benson, reading his thoughts. "Better transfer Mrs. Bobbsey and the younger twins to our boat. We'll take Nan and Bert too, if you like."

Mr. Bobbsey decided swiftly.

"I'll keep Nan and Bert with me. They can swim. I'll need them to help bail," he said. "But you get in Benson's boat," he added to Mrs.

56

Bobbsey. "Freddie and Flossie, you too. Hurry, now! There's no time to be lost!"

The chubby children scrambled over the side of the rowboat. Freddie was in such a hurry that he lost his balance and sat squarely in Miss Higgin's lap.

As Mrs. Bobbsey prepared to follow, the leaky boat listed sharply under her weight. For a moment it seemed as though the unsteady craft would surely tip and fling them all into the water. Mr. Bobbsey put out a hand to steady his wife, however, and Jack Benson gripped her wrists and drew her to safety.

"Now, unless you and Nan and I want a ducking, Bert, we will have to get busy," said the twins' father. "Is there anything to bail with back there? I thought I saw a couple of cans when we got in the boat."

"Yes, here they are—been used for bait, I guess," said Bert, drawing forth two old, rusted tins.

"Well, we'll put them to better use," said Mr. Bobbsey. "Get busy, you two, with the bailing, while I row."

"Will you be all right?" called Miss Higgin anxiously. "There's room for you all in our boat, I think."

Mr. Bobbsey shook his head as he bent to the

oars. "I'm afraid we'd only sink you, also," he said. "Don't worry about us. We'll be all right."

The water was fairly deep in the bottom of the leaky boat by this time. Nan propped her feet on the opposite seat to keep them from getting any wetter. With the empty bait can she bailed energetically. Behind her Bert already was hard at work, splashing the water with little angry plops over the side of the boat.

"Good work," said Daddy Bobbsey, working hard, too. "You're getting it out faster than it's coming in, and that's a help. Lucky the shore isn't too far away."

"Do you think the lake is very deep here?" asked Nan, panting a little from her exertions.

"I can't see bottom," he replied.

To tell the truth, her father was worried. The water in the boat was gaining slowly but surely, in spite of the best efforts of the twins. If the boat should sink, it would mean not only that the three of them would have a long swim and be soaking wet, with no chance to get dry clothes, but also that Hans Weser probably would expect Mr. Bobbsey to pay for the lost boat. He took out his pocket handkerchief, rolled it into a ball, and threw it to Bert.

"If you can see where the leak is, stuff that into it," he instructed.

"I'm not sure, but I think the leak is here, right under where I'm sitting," said Bert. With his knife he wedged the handkerchief into a narrow seam between two of the warped floor timbers. Then he set to work again with his bailing tin.

After that Nan and Bert found their task easier. They really saw that they were gaining on the water. A few minutes later their cans scraped against the bottom of the boat, and they knew the battle was won.

"We're all right now," said Daddy Bobbsey.

Just the same, it was good to be on dry land again. While they stood on shore waiting for the others to come up they discussed the problem of what should be done with the leaky boat.

"I think we will let Jack Benson tow it back to the dock," said Mr. Bobbsey. "I imagine it will keep afloat as long as no one is in it."

"What will *we* do?" asked Nan.

"Walk," said Daddy Bobbsey, smiling at her.

And that is just what they did. The rowboat was tied to the one Jack Benson had hired and was towed back to the dock while Nan and Bert and their father followed on foot.

It was a long walk, and the travelers were hot, dusty, and rather out of sorts by the time they reached the dock. It did not increase their good nature to find Hans Weser already there. The

Hollander was talking with Miss Higgin, her fiancé, and Mrs. Bobbsey, who had just arrived. The twins, Freddie and Flossie, stood close to their mother. Hand in hand, they stared at Hans Weser fearfully.

"There's that man again. Now I suppose we're in for another scene," grumbled Bert.

"There was a leak in the boat," Mrs. Bobbsey was saying as the three who had walked came up to the group. "My husband and two children might have been drowned."

"You are the first person to complain of my boats, Madam," said the Dutchman sourly. "They are good boats. I have not had any trouble with them before."

"I am afraid you will have trouble with them in the future, Herr Weser," said Miss Higgin very firmly. "Your boats are old and I am afraid not very seaworthy. Ours sprung a leak too. Fortunately, it did not do so until we had nearly reached the dock."

Hans Weser grew red. He swelled up until it seemed as if he would burst. He sputtered as he shook a trembling finger at Freddie and Flossie.

"If your boat sprung a leak, then it is the fault of those children," he cried. "They are mischievous children. They make trouble for me, nothing but trouble. If your boat sprung a leak, then I say to you it is their fault. They are responsible for it."

"Oh, nonsense!" said Miss Higgin impatiently. "They are lovely children. I am so fond of them that I am going to have them in my wedding party."

"Oh, so you are going to have them in your wedding party," Herr Weser cried. Again he grew red and swelled up so much that this time Freddie was *sure* he was going to burst! "Well, it is your party, Miss Hester, and so you can do what you like at it."

"Thank you," said Miss Higgin with an angry laugh.

"But you mark my words," said Herr Weser, rising on his toes and shaking his finger at her, "if you have these children at your wedding party they will ruin everything. They will get tangled up in your wedding dress, they will pull apart your bridal bouquet. One of them will fall in your wedding cake. You watch! It will be as I say. They will ruin it all!"

With this awful prophecy and another shake of his finger at the awed twins, Hans Weser departed.

"Golly, I hope we don't do all that!" said Freddie with a sad shake of his head.

"Horrid little man!" said Miss Higgin.

"Quite a character, and one who has never learned to control his temper," observed Mr. Bobbsey.

"A little batty if you ask me," returned Jack Benson inelegantly. "Don't let him worry you, dear," he added to his bride-to-be.

"Oh, I won't. Nobody pays any attention to Hans Weser," said Miss Higgin. Though she shrugged her shoulders and laughed, the Bobbseys could see that she was still angry and disturbed by what the Dutchman had said. After all, no bride likes to be told that her wedding is going to be a failure!

The grown-ups and the children talked for a little while longer and then parted, after promising to meet again soon for a wedding rehearsal.

The twins were quiet during the ride home. Daddy and Mother Bobbsey thought they were just tired, and so, believing that one of Dinah's good dinners would make them all right again, left them to their own thoughts.

The children were tired, it is true, but they were a little bit more than that. They were upset and worried by what Hans Weser had said about them.

In the garden after dinner they talked it all over. Snap, their old dog, was lying contentedly on the grass near them while Waggo roamed rest-

lessly over the lawn until he found in the soft dirt
of a flower bed a bone which he had buried there.

"I wouldn't want to spoil Miss Higgin's wedding," said Freddie, reaching out to pull old
Snap's silky ear. "And I do seem to get into an
awful lot of trouble," he added sorrowfully.

"You don't mean to be naughty, Freddie," Nan
consoled her little brother. "But of course that
wouldn't make it any better if something really
awful should happen at the wedding."

"No," said Freddie sadly, "it wouldn't."

There followed another long silence which was
broken at last by Bert.

"Maybe we better call it all off," he said.

Flossie thought of the pretty ruffled dress
which she had chosen herself and now was all
ready for the wedding. She sighed. Nan thought
of her apron and Bert of his weather vane. Freddie wondered who would carry the wedding ring.
After another long pause Nan said sorrowfully:

"I guess you're right, Bert. I'll write to Miss
Higgin in the morning and tell her we can't come
to her wedding."

CHAPTER IX

AN UNPLEASANT TASK

THE twins all helped to compose a letter to Miss Higgin, though it was Nan who actually wrote it. It said:

"Dear Miss Higgin,

We are sorry not to come to your wedding but we are afraid if we do something will happen to spoil it for you. Freddie is not bad but he is mischievous and he is afraid he might fall in the cake the way Mr. Weser said. Anyway, it would be too bad to spoil your wedding.

We hope you will be happy and we think you will. We like Mr. Benson very much.

Yours lovingly,

The Bobbsey Twins."

When the note was finally completed to the satisfaction of them all, Nan placed it carefully in an envelope and gave it to Flossie to mail. The little girl, proud of being asked to do the errand, started out at once for the mail box at the corner.

Two doors away from her own house, however, she was hailed by one of her friends.

"Come in and see my new baby doll," invited the little girl. "She has real eyelashes and she can walk, too. And she has a whole trunkful of pretty clothes."

Flossie hesitated. She knew that she should mail the letter first, before she did anything else, but the baby doll was a great attraction.

"I'll stay only a minute," she promised herself.

Of course, Flossie stayed more than a minute. She stayed more than an hour, and by the time the baby doll had been dressed and undressed some half dozen times, the important letter to Miss Higgin had been forgotten entirely.

Days passed, and in the excitement of the closing of school Flossie forgot about the letter. The other children believed that Miss Higgin had received it, and regarded the young woman's silence to mean that she was content, even glad, perhaps, that they were not coming to her wedding. They fell into a mood of gloom from which nothing could seem to arouse them. Nan folded up the apron with the embroidery needles still sticking in it. Bert gave up work on the weather vane, although it was nearly finished. Freddie put away the ring with which he had been practicing for the wedding party.

"Ah declares to goodness Ah don't know what's come over you chilluns," said Dinah on the day after school had closed. "Anybody'd think as you wasn't promoted or somethin' but Ah knows you was. Cain't you tell ole Dinah what's makin' you look lak you had lost your las' friend?"

"We're all right, Dinah," said Nan without a smile. "Do you know where Sam is?" she added.

"He's done gone downtown," Dinah replied. "Wanted to get a new rake and some fertilizer fo' de garden, so he say. An' speakin' of angels," she added with a chuckle, "ef here he ain't right now!"

Sam Johnson, Dinah's husband, gardener and general handyman, came into the kitchen. He pulled off his battered soft hat.

"Sho' am hot outside," he said. "Was you wantin' to see me, Miss Nan?"

The girl held out a package that was damp and cool to the touch.

"These are my new chrysanthemum plants, Sam. I wonder if you would set them out for me. You know the place we planned for them, right in the middle of the flower bed at the back of the garden?"

"Sure 'nough, Miss Nan, I remembers," said Sam, accepting the bundle. "But don't you want to come an' watch me while I plants them? You was very partic'lar 'bout jest where dey was to go."

"No, you do it, Sam. I don't feel like gardening today," said Nan.

She turned and hurried from the kitchen while Dinah and Sam looked after her thoughtfully.

"She sho' acts queer, lak she didn't have no interest in anything," said Dinah with a shake of her head.

"Chilluns is strange. No use tryin' to understan' 'bout dem. Ain't no use," said Sam wisely.

Dinah was by no means the only one who had noticed the twins' low spirits, their sudden lack of interest in Miss Higgin's wedding, and the preparations for the trip to Windmill Cottage. After dinner that night when they were all in the living room together, Mrs. Bobbsey spoke of it to them.

"I haven't seen your apron for days, Nan," she began. "Have you finished it?"

"Which apron do you mean, Mother?" asked Nan without looking up from her book.

"Why, the one you were making for Miss Higgin as a wedding present. Have you finished it?"

"N-no," said Nan. "Not quite."

"The time is getting short," her mother told her. "The wedding is only a few weeks off now. Don't you think you should be working on the apron instead of reading a book?"

"Yes—I suppose so," agreed Nan, but not as though she cared very much one way or another.

Mrs. Bobbsey exchanged a puzzled glance with her husband. He cleared his throat, and said:

"How about your weather vane, Bert? Getting along all right?"

"Yes, sir," returned the boy. He was looking at a boys' magazine and continued to turn the pages idly.

"All finished?" asked Mr. Bobbsey.

"Why no, not quite, Dad," said Bert uncomfortably. "You see—"

"Well, son?" prompted Mr. Bobbsey when he had waited in vain for Bert to finish the sentence.

"There didn't seem to be much use in finishing it—"

"Why?" asked Mr. Bobbsey patiently.

"Because—because we're not going to the wedding," blurted out Bert unhappily. "We've made up our minds not to go."

"I might fall in the wedding cake," said Freddie sadly.

"You might—what?" asked Mrs. Bobbsey, not understanding.

"Fall in the wedding cake," repeated Freddie. "Mr. Weser said I would and I guess Miss Higgin wouldn't like it. So—so we decided not to go to the wedding."

"Oh, that's it!" Mr. Bobbsey smiled behind his newspaper and cleared his throat loudly. Freddie wondered if his daddy would like a drink of water. He was just about to ask him when his mother said:

"Does Miss Higgin know about this? Have you told her you won't come to her wedding?"

"We wrote her a letter nearly a week ago," Nan confessed. "Flossie mailed it."

At mention of her name Flossie, who had been curled up in a corner of the couch busily dressing her doll, looked up.

"I didn't mail the letter," she announced calmly. "I lost it."

"You *what*?" demanded Bert and Nan together.

"I meant to mail it," Flossie explained. "But I stopped to see Grace's new baby doll and afterward I looked for the letter and couldn't find it. I must have dropped it somewhere."

"Well!" Nan sat back in her chair and stared at her little sister accusingly. "And all this time we thought Miss Higgin had the letter and that she knew we weren't coming to her wedding. Flossie, why didn't you tell us?"

"I forgot," said the little girl. She hung her head and two big tears dropped on her dolly's blue dress. "I'm awful sorry, Nan."

"Cheer up, Fat Fairy." Daddy Bobbsey lifted Flossie in his arms and set her on his knee. With his own big soft handkerchief he wiped the tears from her face. "Of course you should have mailed the letter because you promised to do it. But since the accident happened, I think it's all for the best."

"Do you mean you are glad Miss Higgin didn't get the letter?" Bert demanded.

"Yes. That is," added Daddy Bobbsey, "if you still want to go to her wedding."

"Oh, we do!" the twins said in chorus.

Mr. Bobbsey smiled at his wife and Mrs. Bobbsey nodded understandingly.

"Then why not go on with your plans for the wedding just where you left off?" their daddy suggested. "Forget you ever wrote the letter."

"And go to Tuliptown and Windmill Cottage and everything?" asked Nan joyfully. "Just as though nothing had happened?"

"Nothing *has* happened," Daddy Bobbsey pointed out. "Miss Higgin didn't get your letter, so she expects you at her wedding. And the rooms at Windmill Cottage are all engaged, you know."

"Hooray!" cried Bert, dropping his magazine. "Gee, Dad, that's great! I'll start work on the weather vane again. It's almost finished anyway."

"And I'll get my apron," cried Nan. She

stopped on her way to the door to hug her little sister and whisper, "Flossie, I *am* so glad you didn't send that letter!"

"There's just one thing," said Daddy Bobbsey gravely. "If you do go to Miss Higgin's wedding your mother and I expect you to behave properly. You must try to make us feel proud of you."

The children promised to do their very best. From that time on they were very happy, and preparations for the wedding and trip to Windmill Cottage went forward as before.

The following day Bert was putting the finishing touches to his windmill weather vane when a shadow fell across his work bench. He looked up to see Charlie Mason standing in the doorway of the garage.

Charlie and Bert were great friends. They were about the same age and had played together and shared adventures as only real chums can do.

"What you got there?" asked Charlie, regarding Bert's handiwork with interest. "Say, I bet I can make one like that. Mind if I take home your windmill and look it over?"

Bert gave his consent, although he did not want to. He insisted on going with Charlie to the basement workshop in the Mason house.

"We start for Tuliptown day after tomorrow," he explained to his friend. "I wouldn't want anything to happen to the weather vane before that."

"I'll be careful," Charlie promised.

But then something happened! On the next to the last step of the cellar stairs Charlie tripped on a loose board and pitched forward. The precious weather vane was jerked from his hand and fell with a clatter to the floor. Poor Charlie fell too—but on top of the weather vane!

CHAPTER X

SPEAKING OF MIDGETS

IT must be admitted that for a moment Bert felt more concern for the weather vane than for the fate of his chum. He pulled the boy to his feet and bent over the windmill.

"Gee, Bert, I'm sorry," Charlie apologized, brushing dust from his clothes. "Did I break it?"

"Not much, I guess," said Bert, trying to be generous. "There's a piece off the bottom and one of the wheel blades is loose. I think I can fix it, though."

The Mason boy had a very complete set of tools and soon the two lads were busily and happily engaged in repairing the damage to the mill. When it was finished Bert had to admit that his weather vane looked even better than it had before the accident!

Meanwhile, everything at the Bobbsey house was in a state of excitement due to last-minute preparations. Trunks and bags had to be brought down from the attic and carefully packed. Socks, handkerchiefs and other odds and ends were always getting lost and turning up in odd places. Through it all everybody was happy, for the long-awaited vacation at Windmill Cottage was soon coming true.

The great day came at last when the Bobbseys were to leave. The trunks had been sent on ahead, so only the suitcases remained to be packed into the back of Daddy Bobbsey's big car. The children ate their early breakfast absently, with one eye on the clock, for they were in a great hurry to be off.

After the meal they said good-bye to Snap and Waggo. Freddie lingered behind the others to promise the little fox-terrier that he could go along on their next trip. Snap followed them to the door, waving his tail politely and smiling at them as a gentlemanly dog should do.

"Yas'm, Ah'll take good care of everything," Dinah promised as Mrs. Bobbsey stopped for a moment in the kitchen. "You don't have to worry 'bout nothin', no ma'am. Sam an' me, we'll git along all right."

Daddy Bobbsey had started the engine, and was ready to go, when Nan recalled that she had left her apron wedding present in the house.

"I'll have to get it, Daddy," she said, scrambling out of the automobile. "I think I know just where it is. I'll be back in a minute."

Nan had finished the apron the night before. She had placed it very carefully in a white box lined with tissue paper, arranging the embroidered corner so it could be seen plainly. The outside of the box she had wrapped in tissue paper too, and tied it with a dainty satin bow. She could remember the very place where she had put it, on an end table near Daddy's favorite big chair.

Nan went to the table expecting the package to be there. But it was nowhere in sight.

"Dinah, my present is gone!" she cried. "Have you seen it? I left it here last night, I'm sure. Oh, where, where can it be?"

"Cain't of gone far, Miss Nan," said Dinah, bustling in. "We'll fin' it, never fret." The two looked all around. There certainly was no package in sight. Finally Dinah called to her husband. "Sam," she ordered, "you go down an' go through dem newspapers in de cellar. Look for a little flat package tied wid a big white bow."

"But the newspapers, Dinah, and in the cellar, too," protested Nan. "How could my present get down there?"

"I fin' de queerest things down 'mong dem newspapers, Miss Nan," Dinah answered with a broad grin. "You'd never s'pect what all Ah finds. Once it was a fountain pen an' once it was one of Mist' Bert's skate keys. All sorts o' things gits mixed up wid dem papers. You wait an' see."

Sure enough, that was just where Sam found Nan's wedding present for Miss Higgin! It had been mixed in with the evening newspapers and carried down to the cellar during the last-minute clearing up before bedtime. Nan accepted the package thankfully, said good-bye again to Sam and Dinah, and ran out to the auto.

"I found it," she said breathlessly. "Sorry to have kept you waiting, Daddy."

Mr. Bobbsey smiled at his daughter. Bert pulled her into the car and slammed the door. Then the Bobbseys started on their way to Windmill Cottage.

The weather was perfect for the trip, the roads good, and the automobile in top form. By noon time they had covered more than half the distance to Tuliptown. They stopped for luncheon at a wayside inn. As they entered the dining room a young lady at a nearby table looked up and smiled at them. She was Hester Higgin!

Mr. and Mrs. Higgin, her parents, were with her. When they saw the Bobbseys they insisted that another table be placed beside theirs so that they all could eat their meal together.

Needless to say, the children were on their

best behavior. Miss Higgin, for her part, seemed to have forgotten what Hans Weser had said about the twins. She talked to the children gaily of plans for her wedding.

"Do you think you will be able to carry the wedding ring without dropping it, Freddie?" she teased. "I think we should have an extra one, just in case," she added with a laugh.

"Oh, no, I won't drop it," the little boy assured her. "I've been practicing awful hard. And I won't fall in the wedding cake either," he added earnestly.

"In that case you would have to fall up instead of down," said Miss Higgin with a laugh, "for the cake will be sitting on a table."

"Well, I couldn't very well fall up," said Freddie and sounded so relieved that everybody laughed.

During the entire meal the children were almost painfully mindful of their manners. Freddie and Flossie were very careful about the way they held their forks. Nan and Bert broke off very small pieces of their rolls one at a time, just as their mother was always telling them to do.

In the end it was Daddy Bobbsey who made a mistake. Turning to answer a question put to him by Mr. Higgin, he knocked against the waiter's arm and sent a portion of ice cream flying through the air. With a sticky plop the dish landed, face downward, on the floor! The twins' father had to admit that he had not behaved as well as his children. Then they all laughed, as he ordered more ice cream.

When they came out of the restaurant the Bobbseys were surprised to find a young man seated on the running board of their car. The stranger was not more than nineteen or twenty, the children thought. His clothes were shabby and dusty and he looked very tired. He got up when they approached.

Mr. and Mrs. Bobbsey with the smaller twins had lingered to speak to Miss Higgin and her parents. The strange young man glanced at them, then at Nan and Bert, who had come up to the car and were regarding him curiously.

"This your auto?" he asked.

Bert and Nan nodded without speaking.

"I suppose you are wondering why I don't take myself off," the youth continued. "I guess I do look like a tramp to you with the dust of a three-day hike on my clothes. Fact is," he hesitated, then went on quickly, "I was wondering if you folks would give me a lift as far as Tuliptown."

"Tuliptown!" Nan exclaimed. "How did you know we were going there?"

"I heard you say so in the restaurant. I was

having a sandwich and a glass of milk at the table next to yours. I thought if you were going to Tuliptown you might give me a lift. It isn't very far."

"Do you live in Tuliptown?" asked Bert.

"Yes. And I'm sorry I ever left it!" The young man spoke with sudden anger. "I should have known better than to have trusted Hans Weser. His name should be Weasel, if you ask me!" he added.

"Gee, I thought your face was familiar!" said Bert. "Weren't you at the rifle booth in Weser's carnival, the one where people shoot at moving ducks?"

"Sure, I was there. I was the one that handed out the rifles. Did you try a shot?"

"No, but I wanted to," said Bert.

The discovery that he had worked at Weser's carnival made the young man seem like an old friend to Nan and Bert. When they explained the situation to their parents a few moments later, Mr. and Mrs. Bobbsey readily consented to give the fellow a lift.

The family had no reason to regret their kindliness, for the remainder of the trip to Tuliptown was made interesting by the stories the youth had to tell them of carnival life. Freddie and Flossie were especially interested in hearing about the midgets, who were real grown-up people, he said, though they were no larger than children.

"If you rode on the windmill Ferris wheel you surely saw some of them," he said. "The gnomes are all midgets dressed up."

"One of them wasn't any bigger than I am," said Freddie wonderingly. "Is he grown up, too?"

"Yes, he is, if he was at the mill," the young man replied. "There's one midget, a woman, who is even smaller. Weser slapped her once for something she did. She doesn't like him now."

"I guess nobody likes Mr. Weser," remarked Nan.

"He's a man you can't trust. He's cruel and sly. He never forgives a person who doesn't do things the way he wants them done. I could tell you some—" The young man broke off and lapsed into a brooding silence.

After a while Bert asked about the peanut vendor. The young fellow's face cleared and he smiled broadly.

"Oh, Tony's all right," he said. "Some crazy kid backed his horse into the stand, knocked over the roaster, and set all the peanuts on fire. The boy's dad paid for the damage, though, and now Tony has a better outfit than ever."

Freddie and Flossie began to giggle and Bert looked uncomfortable.

"I guess I'm that crazy kid," he said. "And it was my dad who paid for the damage. I'm glad the man has a new outfit, though," he added.

When they reached Tuliptown, which they did about half an hour later, their passenger thanked them for the lift and asked to be let off on the corner of the main street.

"I'll be glad to take you anywhere you want to go," offered Mr. Bobbsey. "Just tell me where you live and I'll drop you there."

"Thank you, sir," said the young man, hesitating. "But you see I have no address just now. Fact is, I'll have to look for a place to stay tonight. I'm out of a job—"

"Why don't you come to Windmill Cottage? We're going there," proposed Flossie, who had taken a great fancy to this Ernest Brown. "Couldn't he come with us, Daddy?"

"Oh no, no thanks," said the young man quickly. "You see, I think I know where I can find a job. In fact, it's a pretty sure thing. But I'll have to stick around Tuliptown to get it."

"Well, if we can do anything for you, look us up at Windmill Cottage," said Mr. Bobbsey genially.

"That's very kind of you, sir, and thanks again for the lift." As the young man turned away he smiled at the children and said lightly, "Have a good time at Windmill Cottage. And I hope you find the treasure."

"Gee, wait a minute! What treasure?" Bert called after him.

"You'll find out when you learn the secret of the old windmill," the young man replied mysteriously. "Ask Grandma Haarlem about it!"

"The secret of the old windmill! Grandma Haarlem," Nan repeated, as Daddy Bobbsey slipped in the clutch and the car moved forward. "What do you suppose he meant by that?"

"Sounds awfully int'resting," said Flossie with a little bounce. "I just know we are going to have a good time this summer."

"Golly, maybe we'll find the treasure," said Freddie. "A real treasure with gold and di'monds and everything!"

CHAPTER XI

A VERY OLD LADY

OF course, what Ernest Brown had said about the secret of the old mill was very exciting. The hints he had thrown out about a possible buried treasure seemed almost too good to be true.

They could scarcely wait to get to Windmill Cottage! Even the quaint houses and crooked streets of Tuliptown did not interest them as much at the moment as they should have. The old mill and its secret were all that mattered.

At last the farm came in sight. Through the trees the children could see the house, shining white in the afternoon light, very pretty and snug looking with its green shutters.

Some distance to the rear of it stood the old mill, weather-beaten and decrepit looking. The children wanted to go to it at once, but Mrs. Bobbsey said that they must not do so without permission from Mrs. Van Doorn.

This lady met them at the door of Windmill Cottage. The Dutch woman was almost as broad as she was tall, and had a jolly fat face with cheeks the color of winter apples. She gave the Bobbseys a warm smile and assured them that any friends of the Higgin family would be welcome guests at Windmill Cottage.

"I have saved my best rooms for you," she said. "They are all on the second floor and I think you will like them."

The rooms, like everything about the cottage, were very clean and neat. Pretty flowered curtains hung at the windows, which had been flung open to the breeze. The beds were much higher from the floor than the ones the children used at home. This made Freddie and Flossie giggle, and Freddie had to be scolded for making a running jump to get on top of his.

Mr. and Mrs. Bobbsey were to have the big front room. Two smaller ones were for the children, with the sisters in one, and the boys in the other.

The twins tried hard to be polite, and to answer Mrs. Van Doorn's kindly questions without showing how eager they were to go outdoors. At last Mrs. Bobbsey told them to run along and amuse themselves, but on no account to go farther away than the windmill.

"We shall have cookies and cocoa soon," Mrs. Van Doorn called after them. "You will surely like that, yes? And maybe I will be able to find a few candies for you, too."

The grounds of the place were very attractive. At the back, hidden by the house from the road, was one of the prettiest gardens the children had ever seen. There must have been dozens of rose bushes, most of them in bloom. Along the borders of the beds were velvety petunias, sweet William and early mignonette.

In a vine-covered arbor at the back of the garden sat a very old lady, a black cat curled up in her lap. The children were about to pass by her on their way to the mill when she called to them.

"I know where you are going," she said with a wise nod of her head. "You are on your way to the old mill. Wait a moment," she added, getting to her feet while the big black cat jumped lightly to her shoulder, "and I will go with you."

The twins would rather have inspected the mill by themselves, but they were much too well-mannered to tell the old lady so.

"You have a very nice cat," Flossie said.

"I like black cats," Freddie added.

"Yes, Dykie is a good pet," said the old lady, who walked with difficulty. She leaned heavily on her cane. "He lives at the mill and catches mice.

Yes, yes, Dykie is a good cat. He keeps the mice out of the grain."

Bert and Nan were quite sure, from what they had heard about the mill, that it was old and run-down, and had not been in use for a very long time. In that case, of course, there would be no grain to attract the mice and so no reason for Dykie, the cat, to live there.

Everything was very odd and mysterious. The twins began to feel a little as if the bent old lady with her crooked stick and the big black cat on her shoulder had come to life out of a fairy book.

When they reached the mill they stopped and looked at it curiously. The building itself was made of wood. It had been painted red once, but the paint had peeled off. The storms of years had battered the old boards until now they were a dismal brownish-gray in color. Two steps leading up to a door were cracked and broken, while the old door itself sagged on its hinges. The big wooden wheel creaked and groaned as the after-noon breeze played through its broken blades.

The old lady sat down on a tree stump before the mill and the black cat leaped nimbly to her lap. She stroked its glossy fur and with a trem-bling hand pointed her stick at the old building.

"There it is," she cried in a high voice. "The old mill of the Haarlem family. But it is not what it was when my husband was alive. No, no. Now he is gone and my son is dead too. Whether my grandson lives or not, no one knows. I have not heard from him since he went to war."

"Are you the lady known as Grandma Haarlem?" said Nan. She asked the question timidly for, like the other children, she was a little in awe of the odd old lady.

"Yes, I am Grandma Haarlem. Windmill Cottage belongs to me, but I am an old woman and cannot live alone, so I have rented it to Mrs. Van Doorn. She takes in summer boarders to make money. She is a kind woman. She has been very good to me."

Suddenly as Bert looked at the little old lady he remembered what Ernest Brown had said. "You will find out about the treasure when you learn the secret of the old mill. Ask Grandma Haarlem about it." That was what the young man had said. Bert wondered if he dared take the fellow's advice. Suddenly the lad made up his mind.

"I suppose people always tell stories about old places like this mill," he began. "I guess most old places *do* have secrets—"

"What kind of secrets?" asked the lady quickly. Her eyes were very keen and bright as they looked up at the boy.

"I don't know," Bert confessed, then rushed on. "I thought maybe you would tell us. There is a secret about the old mill, isn't there?"

"Yes, yes, there is a secret, although of course it is no secret to me," said the old lady. She was silent for a few moments and then looked up at the children with dancing eyes. "Would you like to hear a story?" she asked.

"About the mill?" asked Nan.

"About the buried treasure?" said Freddie and Flossie together.

"Yes, it is a story about the old mill and about the treasure too, if you like," returned Grandma Haarlem. "Though of course we are not sure the money is buried here," she added thoughtfully.

"*What* money?" asked Freddie impatiently.

"My grandson had a great deal of money," the lady began. "Nobody knows just how much, but it was the common belief that he was a wealthy man."

"Did he die?" asked Nan.

"No, at least not then. He went away to war, but before he left he worried a great deal about what he would do with his money. He was always a great one for holding on to what he had," she added, chuckling.

Grandma Haarlem paused to smile over her memories. She stroked the fur of the big black cat, whereupon Dykie stretched out in her lap and began to purr cozily.

"Well, to make a long story short, my grandson drew out all his money from the bank, as much of it in gold as he could, and buried it."

"In the old mill?" asked Nan.

"Close to it, anyway," nodded Grandma Haarlem. "I suppose he expected to dig it up when he came back from the war, but he never did return. So now you see why it is that no one really knows where his wealth is hidden."

"Golly! Didn't you ever try to find it?" asked Freddie excitedly.

"Oh yes, many times," nodded the old lady. She leaned toward them and said in a queer voice, "My grandson tells me where to dig!"

"I thought you said your grandson never came back from the war," Nan faltered.

"No, he never has," said the old lady, nodding and smiling. "But I hear his voice sometimes, telling me where to dig. But I have never found anything yet, not a single penny," she added regretfully.

Suddenly Flossie cried out and ran over to Nan, hiding her face in her sister's dress.

"I saw a mouse," she sobbed. "It ran right over my foot!"

At the same moment Dykie leaped from his mistress's lap and darted after the hapless mouse. Grandma Haarlem, startled, let her cane fall with a clatter to the ground. Then from the windmill came an eerie sound like a low moan.

"It is my grandson's voice!" cried the old lady, pulling herself to her feet. "He is telling me where to dig. Give me my spade! Hurry!"

CHAPTER XII

THE TREASURE

FREDDIE saw an old spade leaning against the mill. In a moment he reached it, and ran back with it to Grandma Haarlem.

"I'll dig for you," he offered eagerly.

"Over here," said the old lady. She hobbled away for a few paces, then pointed to the ground at her feet. "Dig here!" she cried. "Hurry!"

Freddie went to work with a will. The ground where Grandma Haarlem had told him to dig had been softened by recent rains, and he found no great difficulty turning over the earth with the sharp edge of his spade.

The old lady hovered over him, sometimes giving him directions and always urging him to hurry. Nan, Bert and Flossie came closer to watch the work. Dykie returned from a vain pursuit of the mouse, and sat down to look on. He had the bored expression of a cat who does not intend to become excited, no matter what happens.

Freddie continued to dig in the soft earth for what seemed a long time to him. His new shoes were covered with dirt and his arms were beginning to ache from wielding the heavy spade. Suddenly he caught the gleam of gold!

Down on his knees went the little boy. He forgot all about his clean white suit, and began to dig in the earth with eager fingers. A moment later he held up, for the inspection of Grandma Haarlem and his brother and sisters, a round gold coin.

"Look!" he gasped. "I've found the treasure!"

"Give it to me!" cried the old lady, grasping the money.

At the same moment a gust of wind struck the mill wheel. It moved a little, and seemed to groan. Grandma Haarlem looked up, smiled, and nodded her head.

"Your voice has directed me to the treasure, Grandson," she said. "I have found it at last!"

Everything was very spooky. To make matters worse there came a sharp flash of lightning and the rumble of thunder.

The children saw that rain clouds were piling up. The wind had risen, too, and over the whole country-side was spread the weird, greenish-yellow light which comes just before a thunderstorm.

The twins had been too intent on the search for

treasure to notice the sky. As they now hesitated, undecided whether they should continue to look for gold pieces or to dash for the shelter of the house, a fresh gust of wind struck them. This was followed by a sharp patter of raindrops.

A voice called, "Grandma Haarlem! Grandma Haarlem! Where are you?"

Of course it was silly of them, but the children had heard and seen so many strange things during the past hour that they half expected some shadowy form to appear in the shape of the ghost of Grandma Haarlem's departed grandson! They were relieved when the short, sturdy figure of Mrs. Van Doorn came from the rose garden and ran toward them.

"Grandma Haarlem, you will get cold," scolded the good woman. "How many times have I told you not to stay out here when the sun goes under a cloud and the air is damp and cool. Come, it is time for your cocoa. You are hungry, yes?"

"I am not hungry in the least," said the old lady crossly. She did not protest, however, when Mrs. Van Doorn threw a light wrap about her shoulders and led her toward the house. By the time they reached the rose garden the rain began to come down in full force. The children scurried to the cottage.

Over their cocoa and cookies they described

their adventure at the mill. When they came to the part where Freddie in turning over the soft earth had actually discovered a gold piece, Mother and Daddy Bobbsey were greatly impressed.

"Where is the money now?" asked the twins' father.

"I gave it to Grandma Haarlem," said Flossie.

"You will let us see this gold piece, yes?" Mrs. Van Doorn asked the old lady coaxingly. "We will tell you how much it is worth."

Rather reluctantly Grandma untied the drawstrings of the little silk bag she always carried, fumbled in its depths for a moment, and then drew forth the piece of money. Though it was full of dirt, they could see that it was a ten-dollar gold piece! The bit of yellow metal was passed from hand to hand, to be examined curiously by each one in turn.

"Was this all you found?" asked Daddy Bobbsey, looking at Freddie.

"Yes. We didn't have time to look for any more, 'cause the storm came. When it started to rain hard we had to run for the house," the little boy explained. "But I'm going back to dig," he added eagerly, "just as soon as the rain stops."

The storm lasted for some time. While the thunder and lightning raged outside and the rain beat against the windows, the Bobbsey family enjoyed the food and the lively conversation of Grandma Haarlem.

The old lady could be very entertaining when she chose. She had been born in Holland and liked nothing better than to tell of her childhood and early girlhood in that charming land.

"Did you wear Dutch caps and aprons and wooden shoes when you were a little girl?" asked Flossie eagerly.

"Oh, yes, we all did," nodded the old lady. "The little girls were very pretty and clean. The boys were sturdy and rosy-faced. We liked best the Christmas season," she added dreamily.

"Then our houses were warm and cozy and they always smelled of bread and cake baking and meat roasting. There was a kind of seed cake my mother made. No one in all Holland could make them so good. People came for miles around just to beg for her recipe."

"Did you see the dykes too? And weren't you afraid that at some time the sea would break in and sweep you all away?" asked Nan.

The old lady shook her head and answered smiling:

"When one is a child, and has lived within the shadow of the dykes always, one doesn't have such fears. Everything is so safe, so solid and enduring in Holland that no one worries about change or danger. It is a beautiful country."

"And then there is always the skating," prompted Mrs. Van Doorn.

"Ah, yes, the skating. There is no skating anywhere such as we have in Holland. There is so much ice. It is hard and lasts a long time. The little girls and boys learn to skate almost as soon as they can walk and after a while it is as natural to them as breathing. Sometimes I can hear again the ring of the blades on ice, the shouts of the skaters as they flash by, the bright, rosy faces of the boys and girls. Yes, it is good to be young in Holland."

The children could have listened to Grandma Haarlem much longer on this fascinating subject, but the old lady suddenly grew weary and began to nod. Mrs. Van Doorn said that it was time for her afternoon nap. The old lady protested feebly, but was taken to her bedroom by the kindly woman.

After Grandma Haarlem had left the room the children made the pleasant discovery that the sun had come out again. The storm, for the time at least, was over.

"I'm going to dig up more treasure," shouted Freddie.

"Put on your rubber-soled shoes if you go out

into the garden," Mrs. Bobbsey commanded. "The ground will be very wet."

The children changed their clothes as fast as they could and ran out through the rose garden down to the windmill.

There was the spade, just where Freddie had dropped it when he uncovered the gold piece. And there was the small mound of dirt and the hole made by his digging.

"We'll all take turns now," Bert decided. "While one shovels, the others can look over the dirt pile to make sure we haven't overlooked any gold pieces."

Under this arrangement the twins set to work with a will. Though they went at it very hard and got themselves very dirty in the process, they saw no glint of gold to reward their efforts. They were forced to admit after a long while that Freddie's gold piece must have been just a lucky find and was not, as they had hoped, part of a golden treasure.

"Cheer up, Freddie," said Bert as they started back to the house to wash before the evening meal. "If Grandma Haarlem knows what she's talking about, there may really be a treasure buried near the mill somewhere. And if there is one we'll find it, never fear."

On the way to the house something jumped out

of the bushes and brushed against Flossie's leg. It was Dykie, who had been forgotten by his mistress. Flossie reached down and stroked the silky fur.

"His coat is wet. I b'lieve he was out in all the storm," said the little girl. She picked the big cat up in her arms and carried him the rest of the distance to the house.

On their way to Tuliptown the next day to do an errand for Mrs. Van Doorn, Nan and Bert met Ernest Brown.

"Hello. Found a job yet?" Bert greeted him.

"Nothing that looks like one," returned the young fellow sadly. "I've been all over Tuliptown but no one wants to employ a person who can't show references. It's back to the farm for me, I guess."

"What farm?" asked Nan curiously.

"My mother's. When my dad died he left her the place and a small life insurance, just about enough to take care of her. That's why I don't want to be a burden to her. See that barn and silo over there?" he added, pointing. "Well, that's where our farm begins."

After talking to Ernest Brown for some time longer the children went on to Tuliptown to do their errand for Mrs. Van Doorn. The shopping took them a little longer than they had expected, with the result that it was nearly noon before they were able to turn back to Windmill Cottage.

"Oh, look!" cried Nan suddenly.

Coming along the road toward them was a monkey not much bigger than Grandma Haarlem's cat Dykie. The little animal was dressed in a red coat and hat. She was laced into a regulation dog harness, from which there dangled a length of leather leash.

"Hello there! Where do you come from and where is your master?" said Nan, kneeling down in the road and holding out her hand to the small creature.

The monkey came closer, chattering and blinking. Suddenly her tiny hand tightened over Nan's finger and she began to jump up and down in the road, whimpering and pulling at her urgently.

"Do you suppose she wants us to follow her?" asked Nan uncertainly.

"Looks that way." Bert picked up the leash and gave it a tug. "Lead on, little Red Jacket," he invited. "If you have a master around here, let's find him."

The monkey needed no second invitation. She seemed to understand what Bert meant, and without wasting any time she started off at a funny ambling gait toward the woods. When she had led them for a little distance she stopped and began to jump up and down again excitedly. A few paces farther on they found the reason for her actions.

A man, probably the monkey's master, lay face downward on the ground. His hands were outstretched before him as though he had been trying to reach something when he fell. The man was an Italian, small and sick looking. His clothes were shabby and covered with dust.

"He lies so still, Bert. Do you think maybe he isn't alive?" Nan asked fearfully.

"I think he's alive all right. Probably just fainted from the heat. Looks half starved, too," said Bert. "Probably hasn't had a square meal in a long time."

"What are we going to do with him, Bert? We can't leave him here."

"That's what we'll have to do, just the same, I guess," Bert decided. "We'll run as fast as we can to Windmill Cottage and send back help from there."

With difficulty they coaxed the monkey to leave her master. The little beast whimpered when they dragged her away. Several times she tried to break loose and run back into the woods but they held her firmly, half leading, half dragging her along the road until they reached Windmill Cottage.

"Better tie the animal in the garden while I go in and telephone for help," Nan suggested, adding with a laugh, "Won't Flossie and Freddie be surprised when they find out what we've brought home!"

As Bert led the monkey around to the back of the house, the little creature gave a sudden jerk and pulled the leash out of his hand. With Bert in pursuit she raced through the rose garden past Grandma Haarlem, who was nodding, half asleep, in the sun. Then she darted in through the open door of the mill.

The old Dutch lady and Dykie, who had been dozing on her lap, started wide awake on the instant. While Bert and the cat ran after the monkey, Grandma Haarlem shook her cane at them and commanded angrily:

"Get that monkey out of there! I won't have such a creature in my mill. Get it out of there, I say!"

Meanwhile Bert raced up the steep, winding stairway in the center of the old mill. Twice he almost got his hand on the monkey's leash, but each time the little pet jerked away just a second too soon.

In the round room at the head of the stairway Bert thought he had the small creature cornered at last. But Dykie slunk toward her, ears flattened and tail waving angrily. The monkey gave a scream of rage and fear and darted through a hole in the rotted boards of the wall, landing on one of the blades of the mill wheel.

Without an instant's hesitation Bert followed her!

CHAPTER XIII

THE MILLWHEEL TURNS

GRANDMA HAARLEM, watching from below, saw the monkey jump to the blade and cling there, chattering angrily. A moment later she caught sight of Bert, and guessing what he was about to do, she screamed out a word of caution.

"Go back!" cried the old lady. "The mill is old and unsafe. The wheel will not bear your weight. Go back!"

Either Bert did not hear the warning, or else he was too intent upon catching the monkey to pay any attention to it. At any rate, he continued to crawl out on the blade. As he felt his way carefully, he spoke in soothing tones to the animal.

The blade was harder to cling to than Bert had thought. The ground seemed to be a long way below when he looked down at it!

The boy closed his eyes and clung tightly until the feeling of dizziness passed. Then he crept on again very slowly, looking straight at the monkey and the dangling leash.

"Go back!" Grandma Haarlem cried again. "The mill wheel is dangerous. You will be hurt!"

By this time Bert had his hand on the monkey's leash. With a quick movement he jerked the little creature to his shoulder. Balancing himself very carefully, he began to feel his way back along the blade toward the mill and safety.

All might have been well had not a sudden breeze chosen at that moment to strike the wheel and turn it ever so slightly. Bert slipped, and for one awful moment it seemed as if he would crash to the ground. However, he was quick and nimble, so he managed to catch the edge of the blade as he fell. He wrapped both arms around it and clung there for a moment while he caught his breath.

Below him Grandma Haarlem seized her cane in trembling hands and hobbled toward the house. Bert knew she had gone to get help. He realized also that whatever help she might bring would arrive too late. If he hoped to be saved, it was up to him to do it!

Carefully the lad edged his way along the blade. His arms were beginning to feel very tired and safety seemed a long way off. The jabbering, scolding monkey, which had felt so light at first became a heavy weight on his shoulder. Bert wondered if the little pet would be able to save herself should the boy fall.

The wall of the mill was very near now. As the panting lad struck it with his arm, he rested a moment. He looked up at the hole through which he must crawl to get inside the building. It seemed a long way above him and for a moment Bert lost heart.

The lad nerved himself to a final effort. He raised up slowly until one knee rested on the blade. Feeling along the side of the mill, he found an uneven place in the boards which his fingers could grip and hold. Then very carefully he stood up on the paddle.

The opening was only about six inches above his head. Hoping that the old boards would hold and that the wheel would remain steady under his feet, Bert gripped the edge of the hole and jumped up.

He got his body half over the opening just as the millwheel began to turn. He saw the blade just above coming toward him! With a last desperate effort he wriggled through and fell to the floor. As he did so, the blade passed the place where his body had been just a moment before!

For a few seconds Bert remained where he had fallen. Beside him the monkey chattered and scolded. A button on the little creature's jacket had come loose and her hat was over one eye. But she could not get free; Bert's hand still clung to the leash.

By this time there were sounds of running feet. The lad heard a disturbance below and then a voice crying anxiously, "Bert, are you all right? Oh Bert, where are you?"

What rejoicing there was when the family found the boy was safe and sound, and that none of Grandma Haarlem's awful predictions had come true. They carried him off to the house where he was petted and pampered much against his wishes. He was given an extra portion of cottage pudding for luncheon.

Everyone listened wide-eyed to the story of his escape. In the end Bert had to promise Mother and Daddy Bobbsey that he would take part in no more reckless adventures of that kind.

The monkey came in for a good deal of attention, especially from Freddie and Flossie, as you may imagine. They soon found that the little creature had been taught to do many tricks. She could dance and catch coins very cleverly in the tin cup which was fastened by a ribbon around her neck.

"Golly, I wish we could keep her. Mayn't we, Daddy?" begged Freddie.

"I'm afraid not, son," said Mr. Bobbsey.

"Then what *are* we going to do with it?" wondered Nan.

This was indeed a question. The owner, who had been found and taken to a nearby hospital at Mr. Bobbsey's suggestion, would not be able to claim the animal for several days at least. Meanwhile, what was to be done with her?

It was not until much later that afternoon that Bert found an answer to the problem. Nan and the younger twins had gone to the Higgins' summer home to talk over arrangements for the wedding, and Bert had retired with the monkey to the rose garden. He was wondering what to do with her when he suddenly thought of Ernest Brown. Why not ask the young fellow to take charge of the little creature for a few days?

The plan seemed so good to Bert that he decided to carry it out at once. He had not gone far when he met Nan and the younger twins, who were returning from their visit to the Higgin family. They were overjoyed at his idea and offered at once to go with him to the farm.

"We can run over to see Ernest now," Nan suggested.

"Maybe Daddy will pay him a few dollars for taking care of the monkey," Freddie added.

"That's right, young fellow," Bert said, giving his little brother a playful cuff on the ear. "It should benefit most everybody; ourselves, Ernest Brown, and the monkey's owner, the poor old organ grinder."

"I think we should go up to the hospital and see that man, don't you, Bert?" asked Flossie. "He must be lonely."

"One thing at a time," said her brother firmly. "We'll get rid of the monkey first."

The children found the Brown farm without any trouble. It was a small place with an apple orchard, a field of wheat, one of corn and some neat rows of vegetables. There was a stable, a chicken house and a silo for stacking grain. These buildings and the house itself were very much in need of paint and repairs.

As the twins approached the cottage they could hear, through an open door, the sound of someone crying in a heart-broken manner. As they hesitated, wondering if they should go on, or choose some other time for their visit, a woman came to the door.

"What do you want?" she asked as they stopped at the porch and looked up at her. "If you have anything to sell you have come to the wrong place. I haven't any money."

Nan hastened to explain their errand, adding that the children wanted to offer her son a job.

"It won't pay very much but it will be better than nothing until he finds something else to do," she said.

Mrs. Brown's expression had softened during this rather long speech. In the end she opened the screen door and invited the children into her kitchen.

A young woman was sitting in a chair near the table. As the children entered she wiped her eyes hastily and turned away from the light to hide the fact that she had been crying. She was not quick enough, however, to avoid Nan recognizing her. She was the same person who had been in charge of the candy and tulip bulb booth in Hans Weser's carnival!

"Why, Miss Juliana, it's nice to see you again," the girl said, going up to the table and holding out her hand in a friendly way. "I don't suppose you remember me, but I'm Nan Bobbsey. You sold me a box of candy at Hans Weser's carnival and we talked about Tuliptown. Remember?"

"Why yes, of course I do. You are one of the twins who is going to be at my Cousin Hester's wedding?"

"Yes," said Nan, delighted that the girl remembered her. "And these are my brothers, Bert and Freddie, and my little sister Flossie."

"Freddie and I are going to take part in Miss

Higgin's wedding," said Flossie importantly. "I am going to be the flower girl."

"And *I* am going to carry the ring," added her twin, strutting a little.

Miss Juliana smiled. "I am sure you will have a lovely time," she said, her voice breaking. Her eyes filled with tears and again she reached hurriedly for her handkerchief. "I'm s-sorry to be so foolish but I c-can't seem to help it. I'm ashamed to be such a b-baby."

The children felt very uncomfortable, for they were afraid it was something they had said that had caused Miss Juliana to cry again.

"Perhaps we shouldn't have mentioned anything about the wedding," said Freddie remorsefully.

"I'm awful sorry," added Flossie.

"Oh, I'm not weeping about that. It's just that everything has turned out so badly. I had a job and was making pretty good money—"

"At Hans Weser's carnival?" asked Nan.

Miss Juliana nodded, dabbing at her eyes. "But nobody can please that man," she burst out angrily. "He is the most hateful person I have ever met. He was always finding fault with me over such little things. And then one day he hinted that I had failed to ring up some of the sales on the cash register. It was the same as saying that I was a th-thief. So I told him I wasn't going to stay there any longer."

"I don't blame you a bit," said Mrs. Brown, resting her hand kindly on the girl's bowed shoulders. "There's no reason for you to feel so bad over it, Juliana. No one can get on with Hans Weser. Even my Ernest had to leave him, much as he needs work."

"Yes, but now I have nothing to do and I *must* get a job," said the young woman desperately. "I have no money and nowhere to go."

"There, there, my dear, don't take on so. You know very well you can stay here as long as you like—that is, as long as we have a roof over our own heads," added Mrs. Brown grimly.

"That's just it. I know how you must feel, being sick so much and with all those doctor's bills to pay. And now with Ernest out of a job—" Miss Juliana broke off and began to sob again forlornly. "I just don't know what is going to become of us all!"

"Oh, I have an idea!" said Flossie, clapping her hands. "I think I know what you can do, Miss Juliana."

The young woman dried her eyes and tried to smile at the little girl.

"Do you, dear?" she asked.

"Can you sew?" asked Flossie eagerly.

"Oh yes, I can do all kinds of needlework. My mother taught me to sew a fine seam when I was a little girl not much bigger than you are now."

"Well, then, you can help Mother finish our summer dresses," said Flossie, clapping her hands again and dancing about in her excitement. "I heard her say just this morning she wished she could find somebody to do it. Don't you 'member, Nan? You were there."

"Flossie's right," Nan said eagerly. "I believe Mother does need somebody to help her, Miss Juliana. If you like we will speak to her about it."

"Oh, I wish you would. You don't know what a difference it would make to me to have some work to do. Perhaps I could even pay Mrs. Brown for board and that would help us all out."

The twins promised to speak to their mother, and to bring word of her decision as soon as possible. Mrs. Brown went with them to the door and presented each of them with a freshly-baked gingerbread cup-cake.

"I will tell Ernest about the monkey," she promised, "and I am sure he will be willing to keep it for you until the owner is well again. You are good children," she added, a softened look on her tired, lined face. "I am glad you came today for Miss Juliana's sake. She needed you."

On the way to Windmill Cottage the Bobbseys

worried a little for fear they might have promised too much on their mother's behalf. They need not have worried, however, for she was greatly interested in the story of the young woman and agreed to do all in her power to aid her.

"I just knew you'd say that!" cried Nan, giving her parent a grateful hug.

"We'll run over the very first thing in the morning and tell Miss Juliana the good news," added Flossie.

"I'll take you over in the car if you like," offered Mrs. Bobbsey.

"Golly, that would be swell, Mother," cried Freddie.

In the morning Nan suggested that they stop at the Higgins' house on their way to the farm.

"Miss Juliana is a relative of the Higgins, you know," the girl said. "Maybe they would be willing to do something to help her."

"A very good idea!" said Mrs. Bobbsey gaily. "We'll stop there first, by all means."

The Higgins greeted the Bobbseys cordially.

"I don't know whether you will be able to find a place to sit down," laughed the bride-to-be, whisking a pile of filmy silk things from a chair. "I am having more fittings today but I am afraid my clothes will never be ready in time for my wedding."

"Do you think you will need some help?" asked Flossie eagerly.

"I am afraid my seamstress will," smiled Miss Higgin. "She is horribly overworked, poor woman."

"Well then, we know the very person who can help her," Nan cried.

"You do? Who is she?" asked Miss Higgin. "If she lives near here she can have all the work she wants."

"Ooh, how perfec'ly lovely!" cried Flossie, clapping her hands. "Let's go over right away and tell Miss Juliana about it!"

"My cousin Juliana!"

"Yes," said the twins' mother. "Would you like to come with us to see her?"

A few minutes later Miss Higgin was in the car with the Bobbseys on the way to the Brown farm.

"This is like being kidnaped," she laughed. "Won't you please tell me what all the excitement is about?"

Obligingly the children related the happenings of the day before. They spoke of the organ grinder's monkey and of their visit to the Brown farm; of finding Miss Juliana there, of her unhappiness and her desperate desire to get work of any kind.

"Poor Juliana! I think I can finish the story for you," said Miss Higgin soberly. "You felt sorry for my cousin and so you came to me, thinking I might be able to do something for her. Well, I will. There is plenty of sewing to be done on my trousseau for the next few days. After that, well, we will see what we can do."

"Mother is giving her some sewing to do for us, too," said Flossie with a bounce. "Oh, here's the house! And look, Bert, there's Ernest Brown with the monkey!"

With the animal perched on his shoulder, the young man came to greet them. He seemed very glad to see them and himself went to the house, where he announced the visitors to his mother. As they entered the kitchen Miss Juliana came up to Flossie and thrust a package into the little girl's hand.

"For you! A surprise!" she said.

CHAPTER XIV

ERNEST'S GREAT IDEA

"A PRESENT!" sang out Flossie, waving the package above her head and dancing about the room. "A present for me and it's not even Christmas!"

"You better open it," said Freddie, eyeing the bundle hopefully. "It might be something we can eat!"

Flossie perched on a kitchen chair to examine her surprise. The wrapping paper flew in one direction, the cord in another. She opened the box, and with a little squeal of delight pounced on its contents.

"It's a dress!" she cried. "A darling little gingham dress! Look at the white collar and the pretty buttons down the back! And a pocket. It's actu'lly got a pocket!"

Everybody smiled at Flossie's enthusiasm. Each in turn had to look at the dress and exclaim over it as the little girl trotted from one to the other, showing her gift. That is, all except Freddie who looked a little disappointed a moment.

"You haven't thanked Miss Juliana yet, have you, dear?" Mrs. Bobbsey prompted her daughter.

"Oh, I forgot! Thanks ever so much," said Flossie politely. "It really is a perfec'ly lovely dress." Then she went over and gave the young woman a hug.

"I made it for a kind little girl who wanted to help me," Miss Juliana explained. "It was no work at all. I loved doing it."

"Juliana, you should have told us you were in trouble," said Miss Higgin kindly. "The last we heard you had a good position with Weser's carnival."

"I left, Hester. I had to. But I'm lost without work. I must find another job."

"That's what we came to tell you about," said Nan eagerly. "We have work for you, lots of it! Haven't we, Mother? Haven't we, Miss Higgin?"

"And you're to begin at it right away," added Flossie.

The young dressmaker was so happy when she learned how all these good people had planned for her that all she could say over and over again was: "Thank you. I don't know why you are so kind to me!"

Finally Mrs. Bobbsey decided they would get along faster with the work if they really sat down and planned just what Miss Juliana was to do for them.

While Nan and Flossie listened to the talk about materials and styles, Bert and Freddie went outside with Ernest Brown.

"I've been over to the hospital to see the monkey's master," the young man told them. "Tony —that's the organ grinder's name—said he would be glad to have me take care of his pet. He was very grateful to everybody—to you as well as to your father for looking out for him, and to me for being willing to mind his pet. He even said he wants to pay me if he ever should get out of the hospital and is able to work again."

"He doesn't need to worry about that," said Bert. "Dad will be glad to make it all right with you for taking care of the animal."

"Daddy was glad to get the monkey away from Windmill Cottage. I think Mrs. Van Doorn didn't like her very much," Freddie offered.

"Well, you see—" Ernest hesitated, as though not quite sure how to proceed. "It's swell of your dad to want to help us out, and all, but Tony and I in some ways are alike. We want to stand on our own feet. He's worried about the hospital bills, and I—well, I'd like to make my own way if I can. I want to earn money and—I have an idea how it can be done!"

"What do you mean?" asked Bert.

"Golly, I bet it has something to do with the monkey!" cried Freddie.

"How did you guess it?" grinned Ernest. "Now I'm going to tell you my plan, and if you think it isn't any good, I wish you'd say so."

With his back against the barn wall and the monkey on his knee, Ernest unfolded his great idea. Bert and Freddie listened with an interest which changed rapidly to enthusiasm as the young man proceeded.

At last the little boy could contain himself no longer. He jumped to his feet with a whoop of delight.

"Golly, when can we begin?" he cried.

"Right away, if you like. I have most of the materials in the garage. Do you want to start now?"

"You bet!" agreed Bert. "I'm like Freddie. I can't wait to begin."

So it happened that when Mother Bobbsey, Nan and Flossie came out into the yard they found Ernest Brown and the two boys hard at work on something that looked at first sight like a great big packing case.

"What are you doing?" Nan wanted to know.

walking all around this queer object and examining it curiously.

"It's just like a 'normous big doll's house," said Flossie with a skip. "*Is* it a doll's house, Ernest?"

"No, it's a monkey's house, or will be when we get it finished," returned the young man.

"It's to have glass sides and running water and 'lectricity," explained Freddie excitedly. "And Mrs. Monkey is to live in it. Golly, won't it be fun?"

"Is it going to have furniture?" asked Nan.

"Of course!" Ernest Brown smiled at the girl as he hammered a nail in place. "What good is a house without furniture? Mrs. Monkey is going to have all the comforts of home. She deserves them."

The grown-ups were as much interested in the new venture as the children. They agreed that the monkey, when taught to do new tricks and to use the elaborate house, should be a very real attraction. Passing tourists might even be willing to pay for the privilege of seeing her!

"We 'spect to make money, Mother, a lot of money," said Freddie importantly, "so that Tony can pay his bill in the hospital and Ernest won't have to worry any more about a job."

"We must make tickets, I guess," said Flossie,

"IT'S A MONKEY'S HOUSE."

busily planning. "And we'll have to sew a dress for Mrs. Monkey. Oh, it's even better than a doll's house," she added rapturously.

Mrs. Bobbsey, finding that she could not drag the children away from their new toy, readily consented to leave them with Mrs. Brown, promising to pick them up in the car later that afternoon. The twins hardly had time to stop to eat lunch, so busy were they.

The next few days they almost lived at the farm. Every time they saw the house of Mrs. Monkey it was more fascinating to them. As it neared completion, the children could be coaxed away from it scarcely long enough to rest.

The back, front and roof of the house were made of wood. The sides were almost entirely of glass. This arrangement would permit interested sightseers to watch what was going on in the little home.

There was a combination dining and living room, a kitchen and a bedroom. Flossie drew upon her dolls' supplies for furniture. She found that Mrs. Monkey fitted very nicely into the bed of her largest doll.

"I'll give my toy stove and cute little pots and pans for the kitchen," she offered.

Miss Higgin donated a toy piano which she discovered in a corner of her attic for Mrs. Monkey's living room. Daddy Bobbsey came home from a trip to Tuliptown one day with a complete set of living room furniture for the new house.

Bert, who was really very clever when it came to using tools, worked side by side with Ernest Brown all day long, assisting him with the water pipes and the electric wiring. Nan, with Flossie's help, was busy making a complete and stylish wardrobe for Mrs. Monkey.

"I think she should have two bonnets, don't you, Nan?" giggled Flossie one day as they worked away with odds and ends of silk and ribbon from Mrs. Bobbsey's sewing basket. "No real lady can get along with only one hat, can she?"

"Oh, absolutely not," returned Nan with a laugh. "Mrs. Monkey shall have one red and one yellow bonnet and a dress to match each of them. And oh, Flossie, do you remember the toy parasol Mother gave you for Christmas? It would be just the thing to go with the red outfit. Do you think we could teach Mrs. Monkey to use it?"

"I guess so. She's an awful smart monkey, you know," returned Flossie, nodding her head wisely.

Long before preparations had been completed, the fame of Mrs. Monkey and her wonderful house had spread far and wide. Cars began to turn into the road leading to the Brown farm and their curious passengers would stroll up to watch the busy group at work. Seeing all this, Ernest Brown arrived at a quick decision.

"The time has come for us to ask people to pay admission," he said. "These folks are seeing our show for nothing, and that will never do. Bert, you and Nan make out some ticket forms, will you? While you're doing that, Freddie and Flossie and I will stake off our exhibit so that people can't come too close to it without an invitation or a ticket. We'll need a policeman too."

"What for?" asked Freddie.

"Oh, to keep the crowds in order, of course. And Freddie," he added, smiling at the little fellow, "I believe you're it!"

"What am I?" asked the small boy, puzzled.

"Our policeman! Come up to the house while I see if I can find you a uniform," said Ernest Brown.

Freddie hadn't the slightest idea what kind of a policeman he would make. However, when he was all dressed up in a blue suit with brass buttons and had been given a little club to carry, he felt suddenly rather important.

"I guess I won't make such a bad officer after all," he said.

At last the house was finished. Mrs. Monkey, very stylish in a red costume and carrying the gay parasol, was taught a number of difficult tricks. First she would go to the living room, where she would put down her parasol on a couch. Next she would untie the strings of her bonnet and then take it off. Then she would pass through the bedroom and into the kitchen where she would fuss about with pots and pans. After turning on a faucet over a tiny sink from which real water ran out, she would sit down.

This was Flossie's signal to enter the house. This she could do by stooping a little. She would announce to Mrs. Monkey that she had come to tea. After some play eating with a set of doll's dishes, the monkey would shake hands with Flossie and suddenly hustle off into the bedroom, where she would get into bed and pull the covers up to her chin!

At last the day came when the real show was to be opened to the general public. The twins were very excited.

"I hope Mrs. Monkey doesn't forget what we've taught her," said Nan nervously as she helped Flossie get into her grown-up dress in Mrs. Brown's parlor. "Are you ready now, dear? All right, let's go."

When she reached the door Flossie drew back.

"There's a big crowd out there," she said. "I'm kind of scared, Nan."

At this point Freddie, looking very grand in a policeman's uniform, poked his head in at the door.

"Ernest says for you to hurry. It's 'most time for you to take tea with Mrs. Monkey. Come along, Flossie."

The little boy trotted before his sister importantly, clearing a way through the crowd with his stick. Smiles and murmurs of approval followed the little procession. Those who had been lucky enough to get close to the show house watched with interest as Flossie went inside and gravely shook hands with Mrs. Monkey.

Everything went off very well. Mrs. Monkey obliged with her tricks as cleverly as though she had been accustomed to acting all her life. Flossie was sweet and lovely in her part, and Freddie in his role of policeman made a hit with everyone.

Tickets sold like wild-fire. So many quarters soon filled Nan and Bert's little boxes to overflowing that the money had to be emptied into the big tin box of which Ernest had charge.

"It's an even bigger success than we had hoped," commented Nan as she and Bert went back to their task of collecting tickets. "Mrs.

Brown and Miss Juliana are serving tea and cakes on the side porch and have more business than they can attend to. Miss Juliana is talking of opening a tea shop. Why Bert, what's the matter?"

"Listen!" her brother whispered with a hand on her arm, "those two men over there are talking about Windmill Cottage!"

CHAPTER XV

QUEER SIGHTS AND SOUNDS

THE children did not mean to overhear what was being said. However, anything about Windmill Cottage or the old mill was of the keenest interest to them. Therefore, they paused to listen.

"Lots of old buildings are supposed to be haunted," one man was saying. "I don't put much stock in these stories myself."

"The rumors about the old mill are pretty persistent, though," the other replied. "I've heard lots of folks say they have seen strange lights about there at night. Noises, too, and groans, as if somebody were in pain."

"Old Grandma Haarlem is probably responsible for a lot of the queer goings-on," the first man answered. "They say she wanders about the place at night with that black cat of hers looking for something. A peculiar old body she is, a little funny in the head, more than likely."

The two men moved on, and were soon lost

in the crowd. However, they had said enough to renew the children's interest in the ghostly story about the old mill. They decided then and there to look into it more thoroughly as soon as they could get the chance.

Meanwhile, more and more people continued to arrive at the farm, all of them straining their necks for a sight of Mrs. Monkey and her mansion. Nan's tickets were all sold; Mrs. Brown's supply of tea and cakes was gone and still the silver rain of quarters continued. Ernest Brown's tin box was filled to overflowing. By the end of the day everybody who had had any part in the show was completely tired out, but oh, how happy!

"I haven't counted all the money, yet, but we must have taken in a small fortune," said Ernest happily. "If we have many days like this, old Tony and I soon will be rich."

"Our little tea room was a great success too," said Miss Juliana, gathering up heaps of soiled cups and saucers. "All Mrs. Brown's cookies were eaten in no time."

"Why don't you open a real tea shop?" Nan suggested. "The side porch is cool and shady and large enougn to hoid half a dozen tables. If you need more tables to take care of the crowd you can set them out under the trees."

"I think that would be wonderful. I believe we

could make a real success of it," said the young woman thoughtfully. "I'm going to talk to Mrs. Brown about it right now."

"Would you have cookies at the tea shop?" asked Freddie eagerly.

Miss Juliana smiled at him. "Oh, lots and lots," she replied. "And some 'specially fat sugary ones for a little boy policeman. Wait and see!"

"Golly, I don't want to wait. I'd like to start right now!" said Freddie.

For several days the show was a great success. The tea shop was opened, and sold as many cakes and cookies as Mrs. Brown could make. Freddie strutted around in his policeman's uniform and sampled the food, far more of it probably than was good for him. Flossie continued to wear her grown-up dress, taking tea several times each afternoon with Mrs. Monkey.

Just when they were all having the time of their lives and everything was going along beautifully, something happened. Ernest Brown came over to Windmill Cottage one morning to say that the person who had the mortgage on the Brown farm had refused to wait any longer for the money owing to him.

"He has told us we must leave."

The twins were almost as much upset as Ernest was over this unfortunate turn of events. They suggested several plans for helping the Browns and saving the farm, but none of them seemed any good. It was not until the young man had left that Nan had her great idea.

"I wonder if Mrs. Van Doorn would let us move Mrs. Monkey and her house over here?" she suggested. "She was very much interested in the show the day she came to see it."

"And she thought Mrs. Monkey was awfully cute," Flossie added. "Let's ask her."

The twins went together to find Mrs. Van Doorn. The good lady was in her kitchen planning the noon meal. She greeted the children with her usual friendly smile.

"You are hungry, yes?" she surmised. "You would like a little jelly bread spread ever so thin and sprinkled with powdered sugar?"

"Golly, I should say so," said Freddie, climbing on a high stool near the kitchen table. "I'll take two pieces of jelly bread, please."

"Freddie, don't be greedy," reproved Nan in her best "little mother" tone. "One piece of bread and jelly is all you should have."

"I know that, but it *tastes* so good," said Flossie gravely.

"The truth is, we really have come to ask a favor of you, Mrs. Van Doorn," said Bert, plunging into the heart of the matter at once.

"Oh, so?" returned the good lady with her comfortable smile. "What is the favor, then? Come, I am listening."

Thus encouraged, the children told their friend all about Ernest Brown's troubles. They painted a touching picture of the sad future that awaited him and his mother and Miss Juliana, to say nothing of Tony and Mrs. Monkey if something were not done to aid them.

"So! Now I have a very good idea of this favor you are going to ask me to do for you!" Mrs. Van Doorn put two plump hands on her broad hips and regarded the twins sternly. "You are about to say, are you not, that you would like me to have this Ernest Brown and his mother and this one you call Mrs. Monkey to live at my house? That is what you would say, yes?"

"We thought you might not mind," said Nan shyly. "You see, they really haven't any place to go."

"Mrs. Brown makes awful good cookies. She might give you some," said Freddie boldly.

"Ernest could assist your hired man about the place," Bert put in. "If you need any shelves anywhere or any other work like that Ernest could do it. He's mighty handy with a saw and hammer."

"Miss Juliana would help, too," said Flossie.

"She might even make you a dress like the one she made me."

Mrs. Van Doorn's sober face finally relaxed into a smile.

"I would look nice in that kind of dress," she laughed. Then she added hastily, "Well, well, I will not say yes or no to you just now. I will think over what you have said and tomorrow I will give you my answer."

With these few words the twins were forced to be content. The fact that Mrs. Van Doorn had not refused their request outright seemed to them a pretty good sign, and they prepared to await as patiently as they could her final answer on the morrow.

That night Bert was awakened abruptly by a sound that seemed to come from the hall just outside the door of his bedroom. Being careful not to arouse Freddie, the lad slipped from bed, ran to the door, and opened it. At the same moment the one across the hall opened and Nan looked out.

Along the corridor, her hands outstretched gropingly, walked the bent, white-robed figure of Grandma Haarlem. The eyes of the old lady were wide open but they were without expression. She was walking in her sleep!

Nan made a sign to Bert. "Put on your bathrobe and slippers," she whispered excitedly. "We'll follow her!"

Although the twins dressed as swiftly as they could, there was no sign of the old lady when they reached the lower floor. An open door in the kitchen told them she had gone outside. They followed swiftly.

The garden and the rose arbor were empty. Nan and Bert paused for a moment to listen. They could hear the sharp thud of a spade striking against the earth. The sound came from the direction of the old mill!

The children thought of all the ghost stories they had heard about the place, and the strange sights and sounds to be seen and heard there on dark nights. For a moment they hesitated. Then Bert seized Nan's hand and pulled her forward.

As the twins reached the clearing beyond the garden the children came upon a strange sight. Grandma Haarlem was there! Clad in a long white robe, she was a ghostly figure as she bent over her spade in the moonlight and turned back the soft, black earth. Near her was the black cat Dykie.

Nan and Bert were about to run forward when another figure appeared from the darkness. The intruder, a very large man with shoulders as big as a bull, reached Grandma Haarlem in three long strides. He pulled the spade roughly from her grasp and began to dig feverishly at the small hole she had made.

The old lady screamed and with a frantic gesture put her hands to her head. Bert and Nan raced across the cleared space to the mill. They reached the old lady's side in time to catch her as she fell forward in a faint.

Meanwhile the strange man, startled by the sudden appearance of the children, had dropped the spade and run off, leaping the fence to a nearby pasture. At the same moment there was a bellow of rage from Grandma Haarlem's old bull, Sookie. With lowered horns it charged the man who had so rudely disturbed its sleep!

The fellow stumbled and fell to his knees. He staggered to his feet and jumped aside just in time to avoid the goring rush of Sookie's horns. The bull whirled and charged again.

This time the man fled, stumbling and half falling in his haste. He was no match for the bull in speed, and certainly would have been caught and trampled by the animal had it not been for the presence in the pasture of an old maple tree.

The branches of this tree grew close to the ground. The man grasped one of them and swung himself aloft just in time to avoid the punishing horns of Sookie.

CHAPTER XVI

AN ANGRY BULL

"I GUESS that big man is safe enough for the time being," said Nan with a nervous laugh. "Sookie will see that he doesn't get into any mischief for a little while."

"We'd better get Grandma Haarlem back to the house," said Bert.

The old lady, though still weak and shaken, had come to her senses. She submitted meekly when the children lifted her to her feet and led her toward the building.

In the garden they met Emile, the hired man, who had been roused by the shouts and screams and had come to find out about them. Nan and Bert told him of the strange man and Sookie. Emile immediately set out on a run for the pasture.

In Windmill Cottage all the grown-ups had been awakened by the commotion. Mrs. Van Doorn now came to meet Grandma Haarlem and led the frail old lady off to bed, fussing over her anxiously and scolding her for going out in the damp night air. Bert and Nan begged Mr. and Mrs. Bobbsey to go to the pasture to see what was happening.

"What can we do when we get there?" inquired Mrs. Bobbsey of her husband in low tones. "After all, an angry bull is dangerous."

"Emile has been brought up on a farm and I'm certain he'll know how to act," answered Mr. Bobbsey.

However, when they reached the fence which the stranger had jumped so lightly in his hurry to get away, they did not see the bull. He was lying contentedly at the opposite end of the pasture! There was no sign at all of the mysterious visitor. The man, whoever he was, had evidently found some means of escape.

"I'd sure like to know how that fellow got away," said Emile as they turned back. "I guess there won't be any more excitement tonight."

The Bobbseys were sorry that the prowler had succeeded in getting away. They were all indignant at the fellow's brutal treatment of Grandma Haarlem and would have liked to have seen him punished.

When they reached the house Mrs. Van Doorn, always thoughtful of others, made them some hot cocoa. Later, as they were going up-stairs, Bert said to Nan:

"Do you know what I think? I bet that man we saw tonight has something to do with the ghost stories we've heard about the old mill."

"You mean he has spread those stories around so that no one would dare look for the treasure? I've thought of that too, though I haven't the slightest idea who he can be, or what connection he has with Grandma Haarlem and her grand-son."

"He could pretend to be the ghost of her grandson, couldn't he?" Bert argued. "He might even be responsible for some of the spirit mes-sages the poor old lady thinks she hears."

The rest of the night passed quietly enough. It was well along in the morning when Freddie awoke to see the sunshine streaming into the pleasant room he shared with Bert. He quickly roused his brother, and the two, after a friendly pillow fight, were soon dressed and downstairs.

Mother and Daddy Bobbsey and Nan were al-ready at breakfast but Flossie had not appeared yet. When she did come, it was with a clatter of small feet and with cheeks so rosy that she looked like a cherub. Her father swung her high in the air and set her down in a chair at the dining table.

"How's my fat fairy this morning?" he asked.

"I'm fine, Daddy, 'cept I dreamed of bulls all night long; great big ones with sharp horns!"

"What!" said Mrs. Bobbsey.

"I guess it's my fault," said Nan, looking uncomfortable. "Flossie was awake when I came back and I told her about the bull."

To tell the truth, the excitement of the previous night seemed like a dream even to Nan and Bert. They were determined, however, to hunt for the strange man in their spare time.

The younger twins did not eat well that morning. Mrs. Bobbsey, much to her amazement, had to urge them to try their cereal. The fresh eggs gathered early in the day by Mrs. Van Doorn were not touched.

"The hens would be sad if they knew about this," said Daddy Bobbsey.

The reason for this strange lack of appetite soon became known when Freddie, with a glance into the kitchen, whispered:

"Golly, do you s'pose she'll say 'yes'?"

"Well, she almost did yesterday," returned Flossie.

"What are you two talking about?" asked Mrs. Bobbsey.

"I think they're wondering if Mrs. Van Doorn will let the Browns and Mrs. Monkey come over here to live," Bert explained.

As soon as breakfast was over, Flossie and Freddie wandered into the kitchen where Mrs. Van Doorn was busy.

"My two little friends are feeling well this fine morning, yes?" said the jolly Dutchwoman, beaming on them.

"We're fine, but—"

"We'd feel even better if Mrs. Brown and Ernest, and Miss Juliana and Mrs. Monkey could come over and live with us," broke in Flossie. "It would be such an extra-special favor if you'd let them."

Mrs. Van Doorn, hands on hips, stood looking at them, while a smile slowly broke over her broad face.

"The excitement will not be good for Grandma Haarlem, especially after last night, and I know I should not do it. But what is a poor old Dutchwoman, after all, against two such as you? They may come."

With a whoop Freddie was off to tell Nan and Bert the good news. The four little Bobbseys were soon at Mrs. Brown's home, all trying to tell her at once that her worries were over and that now she and Ernest and Miss Juliana could come to live with them.

Of course, if the twins had had their way, the moving would have started that very day, but the grown-ups thought it best to wait a little longer. Moving day finally did come and found the Bobbseys at the Brown farm bright and early, ready to help as much as they could with the preparations.

"We know we'll probably be a nuisance more than anything else," said Nan to Ernest, "but there ought to be some way that we can help."

"Well, I'll say there is," the young man replied. "You know how things collect in the cellar and the attic. Why don't two of you go down to the basement and the other two up to the attic? Look over everything you find. Anything that could possibly be of any use show to me or my mother. If we want to keep it you can take it over to Mrs. Van Doorn's for us."

"I'd love to look in the attic," said Nan eagerly. "One always finds such romantic things there."

"You would think of that," Bert grumbled, "but I'll go with you anyway."

While Bert and Nan climbed the stairs to the top of the house, Freddie and Flossie clattered down into the damp mustiness of the cellar.

"Golly, it's dark here," the little boy murmured.

Flossie gave a squeal of fright as he stumbled over a box that lay in the middle of the floor.

"Oh, look at that big trunk over there. I bet

I'll find just heaps and heaps of nice things in it," cried Flossie.

"While you're looking in that I guess I'll see what's in the back of the cellar," Freddie announced importantly.

The next moment there was a clatter and a bang followed by a thud as Freddie stumbled into the coal bin. When he reappeared he didn't look like himself; his face was now black!

"I found an old spade," he said gaily. "I'm sure nobody wants it. I guess I'll hide it in the old mill just in case Grandma Haarlem loses hers and we need it to hunt for the treasure," he added, trying to rub the dirt off his face and only making it look worse.

Flossie continued to rummage in the old trunk and finally brought to light an odd, battered rag doll. Up the stairs she raced as fast as her fat little legs would carry her. Into the living room she went, where Mrs. Brown was busy making bundles of her more precious belongings.

"Mrs. Brown, do you s'pose, do you just possibly s'pose I can have this?" she asked breathlessly.

"Surely you may have it, Flossie," was the answer. "Have lots of fun with it."

As the young Bobbsey twin went off with the precious doll held close to her, Bert and Nan

came downstairs with an old brown suitcase which
Ernest said his mother wanted to keep. They set
off with it, walking along the path which led from
the farm to Windmill Cottage. They had not
gone far when Nan, happening to glance back,
saw the stocky form and fat face of Hans Weser.
The Dutchman was only a few steps behind them!

"I'm afraid we may have more trouble with
that mean man," she whispered anxiously to Bert.
"Don't look now, but he's coming along right
back of us!"

As she spoke, the old suitcase which Bert was
carrying suddenly opened. Its contents of dresses
and knickknacks spilled right in the path of the
hurrying Weser! He stumbled and almost fell
flat. Flushing with anger, he turned on the twins.
When he recognized them, he became still redder.

"So! More trouble it is that you good-for-
nothing children bring me," he shouted. "You trip
me up, yes? You make me fall in the dirt and
break my back, perhaps, or my neck. What do
you care? Nothing! Get away from me," he cried.

With that he flung himself away. The twins
gathered up the dresses and once again shut the
suitcase. Then Bert said thoughtfully:

"I wonder what Hans Weser is doing here, so
close to Windmill Cottage? I bet he's up to some
sort of mischief."

"Let's follow him for a little way and see where he goes," Nan proposed.

Bert liked the idea of playing detective, so he readily agreed. To do their work right they decided that they must be very quiet so as not to let Hans Weser know they were trailing him.

In a little while he turned abruptly from the road and plunged into the woods. He stopped suddenly at the end of the path among a sheltered grove of trees. The twins came as close as they could without danger of being seen. Weser was already speaking with a very large, muscular person.

"So your name is Herman Klaas," he was saying, "and you want a job in my carnival as a strong man. You claim that you can put on a treasure hunt, yes? Well, first you must prove to me that you are as strong a man as you say you are."

"That will be easy," Klaas replied. "Why, the other night I was chased by a bull, and if he hadn't gone off on his own accord," he boasted, "I could have given him a good fight."

Bert and Nan exchanged glances. So this was the man who had caused all the excitement at Windmill Cottage, and then had disappeared into the night!

CHAPTER XVII

THE TURKEY GOBBLER

WHILE Bert and Nan stood puzzling over this strange turn of events, Klaas continued to boast of his great physical strength.

"Why," he exclaimed, "I sometimes pick up an automobile just for the exercise."

Hans Weser looked as if he did not believe this, and again insisted that he would need some real proof that Klaas could do all the things he claimed before he would hire him.

"So you don't believe me?" said the big man. "Well, if we can find a car somewhere in this lonesome neck of the woods, I'll show you I'm telling the truth."

The twins shrank back into the bushes, breathing sighs of relief when the men failed to see them as they passed by.

"Let's follow them again," whispered Bert. "We may discover something interesting."

When Weser and Klaas had walked perhaps a

quarter of a mile down the road, with the anxious Bobbsey twins following close behind, they came upon a parked car. It was a heavy, seven-passenger automobile but this did not seem to disturb Klaas the least bit.

"Now watch me do my stuff," was his only comment.

The children in their hiding place held their breaths as he grasped the rear bumper firmly with both hands. Nan could hardly keep from crying out, when with no difficulty at all the man lifted the back part of the heavy machine, turning the car completely around so that it faced in the opposite direction!

Weser seemed deeply impressed, as indeed anyone would have been. Smiling as pleasantly as it was possible for him to do, he shook Klaas's hand and exclaimed:

"Well done, my boy, well done. Of course I can use you in my carnival. You will be my main attraction. But what is this, what is this?"

In his eagerness to see and hear all that went on, Bert had leaned too far forward, lost his footing, and crashed through the bush which had hidden Nan and himself. For a moment it seemed as if Weser would burst with anger. He made no effort to control himself.

"I told you that you vould be sorry if ve ever

met again, and you vill be, you little snoops," he said, rushing toward the twins.

"Now hold on," interrupted Klaas. "I don't like the idea of those kids spying on us any more than you do, but it's not going to do any good to beat 'em up, or scare 'em half to death." Then, turning to the Bobbseys, he said, "See here, youngsters, just what is the big idea?"

It was a frightening position for Bert and Nan, two children against two men, one of them very angry and the other certainly not friendly. However, Bert managed to show his courage and spoke to Klaas as boldly as he dared.

"We heard you tell Mr. Weser that you were chased by a bull the other night," he said, sounding braver than he really felt. "So we think you must be the man who grabbed the shovel from Grandma Haarlem and then ran off when she woke up. You had heard about the treasure at the old mill, and were trying to take it away from Grandma Haarlem."

"Why, you — you — crazy kid!" blustered Klaas. "What do you mean, talking to me like that! You better clear out, both of you, before I really lose my temper!"

The twins were glad to follow his advice. They hurried off toward Windmill Cottage, leaving the two men busily engaged in conversation.

Of course the whole affair had to be told and retold afterward for the benefit of Mother and Daddy Bobbsey, who were particularly interested in Herman Klaas. They were inclined to agree with the children's suspicion that he was the same man who had disturbed the peace of Windmill Cottage and frightened Grandma Haarlem.

"He didn't deny it, anyway, when Bert charged him with it," said Nan.

Daddy Bobbsey exchanged a glance with his wife, then said slowly:

"I hate to disappoint you children, but I'm afraid you mustn't count too much on finding a treasure at the old mill."

"Grandma Haarlem is very old, and very old people, like very young people, often imagine things," added Mrs. Bobbsey. "You know how Freddie and Flossie sometimes see wonderful pictures in the clouds. The castles and rivers and trees look real, but we know they are not."

"Then you think Grandma Haarlem only imagines there is a treasure?" asked Bert in a disappointed tone.

During the next few days treasure hunting was forgotten in the excitement of once more exhibiting Mrs. Monkey in her cute little home.

Mrs. Brown and Ernest had been welcomed warmly by Mrs. Van Doorn and were now part of the household. Miss Juliana had been invited to stay with them too, but had accepted instead an invitation from Mrs. Higgin to live with her.

Crowds now flocked to Windmill Cottage, and the many children who came with their parents never failed to be highly delighted and thrilled with the fine show. Many of them paid to see a second performance.

One afternoon while Nan was passing out monkey souvenirs, she saw poor old Grandma Haarlem standing at the edge of the crowd. She gazed wistfully at each new face. Nan hurried over to the old lady.

"Is there anything you want, Grandma Haarlem?" asked the girl. "If there is, just tell me and I'll try to get it."

"I am afraid, my dear, that what I want only God can give me," was the sad reply. "I thought perhaps I might see my grandson among all these people but I guess it is of no use to hope."

Leaning heavily on her cane, she hobbled off. With an ache in her heart Nan again resumed her task of passing out souvenirs.

Later that same afternoon Miss Higgin dropped in at Windmill Cottage to see the Bobbseys. She explained that her real reason for coming over was to invite the children to a picnic at her house the following afternoon.

Flossie clapped her hands and gave a little squeal of delight. "I'll be there!" she said.

"Golly, won't we have fun!" shouted Freddie. "I hope Mother will let us go."

Mrs. Bobbsey was glad to have the twins enjoy the picnic, so it was decided that Daddy Bobbsey should drive them over to the Higgin home early the following day. The next morning a message arrived for Mr. Bobbsey, calling him home on important business.

"Sorry I must take the car but you can go as far as Tuliptown," their father said. "I'll rent bicycles there at a place I know and you can ride up to the Higgin farm in great style."

The children thought this would be fun, although Freddie and Flossie wondered if they could ride such a long distance.

"You must be very careful and always keep close to the side of the road to avoid automobiles," Daddy Bobbsey instructed.

The twins promised, and so were driven into town and provided with four bicycles. The two small ones for Freddie and Flossie were very easy to ride, but even so Flossie was pretty wobbly on hers and Freddie was not much better.

"I'm afraid it's going to take a long time to reach Miss Higgin's house," Flossie panted.

With tongue between her teeth and fat little

legs going just as hard as they could, she was de-termined to keep moving in a straight line, al-though the bicycle seemed to want to run off to right or left. All of a sudden the front wheel turned sharply, the bicycle rolled into a ditch, and Flossie landed in a cloud of dust.

"Are you hurt, dear?" asked Nan, running to her sister.

"No, I guess not," said the little girl uncer-tainly. "But I'm afraid my pretty red dress is all dirty."

However, the dust was soon brushed off and Flossie felt and looked no worse for her tumble. She and Freddie managed to ride the rest of the distance to the Higgin home without further trouble.

Several tables were set up under the trees which here and there dotted the lawn. Not many people had arrived as yet, but the twins did see Ernest Brown. He showed them around in the absence of Miss Higgin and her mother, who were busy in the kitchen.

Near the barn he pointed to a wire pen in which, much to the children's amazement, was a large turkey gobbler. He warned them not to get too close to it.

"It's a wild old bird and has to be shut up when people are around," Ernest explained. "It's especially dangerous when it sees anything colored red."

The bird seemed to be in a particularly bad temper that morning. Maybe it got excited over Flossie's red dress! At any rate, it pecked furiously at the door of the cage and spread its big wings.

All of a sudden it gave a very hard blow with its beak, and the door burst open. The angry turkey gobbler made a dash for Flossie!

CHAPTER XVIII

AN EXCITING CHASE

CRIES of alarm rose from the children as they saw the vicious bird making for the little Bobbsey girl.

"Look out, Flossie!" cried Freddie. "He's coming for you!"

"Run, Flossie, run!" shrieked Nan, fearing for her sister.

Flossie ran as fast as her little legs could carry her. They would not have brought her very far if the gobbler had had a clear path, but by this time Ernest was trying to stop the bird, and it had to dodge and twist to get a view of Flossie's red dress.

Bert was running with all his might to get in front of the turkey and turn its attention to himself. He got only near enough, however, to receive a side blow from the powerful wing of the bird that threw him off his balance.

The boy measured his length on the ground but

was up again in a second to renew the pursuit, his heart beating fast with fear as he thought of what might happen to Flossie should the turkey overtake her. That fear was increased when the little girl tripped over a stone and fell.

A few seconds more, and the turkey would have reached her, when just at that moment Ernest came running, grabbed the bird by the neck, and brought it to the ground. It gobbled with rage and struck out vigorously with its beak and wings, but the young man held on.

By this time others had heard the cries and hurried up. They helped hold the bird, which was dragged off and carried back, still protesting, to the cage from which it had escaped.

Flossie was sobbing with fright when Nan and Bert reached her. Her sister hugged her joyously.

"Are you hurt, darling?" she asked, as she kissed the little tear-stained face.

"No—no," sobbed Flossie, burying her head in Nan's shoulder, "but I was awful scared. Why did it chase me? I wasn't doing anything to it."

"It was your red dress, I guess," replied Nan. "Here's Ernest."

"Thank you, Ernest," quavered Flossie. "You saved my life, I guess."

"Oh, not as much as that," grinned Ernest as he brushed the dust from his clothes. "I've tackled those fellows before out at the farm. Sometimes they're pretty ugly. I guess Bert found that out," he added, as he saw the Bobbsey boy rubbing his leg. "The gobbler gave you a pretty bad blow, didn't he? I've known them to break a fellow's leg with one of their wings."

"I'll bet my leg will be black and blue for a while. I hope Dad will keep an eye on that turkey and buy him for the next Thanksgiving dinner," he added with a grin. "That will be one way of getting even with the old bird for the scare he gave us today!"

A nice picnic lunch helped to restore things to normal, the finishing touch of which was lots and lots of ice cream for the children. Following that, their attention was attracted by the arrival of wedding presents. There seemed to be no end to them, and the number showed how many nice friends Miss Higgin and Jack Benson had.

"My, what a lot there are," murmured Nan, as she viewed the beautifully-wrapped boxes and packages.

"I wish we could open them," said Flossie wistfully.

"Golly, I'd like to help unpack," said Freddie.

"I don't see why you shouldn't all help," said Miss Higgin with a smile. "But be careful, please," she added. Freddie felt a little uncomfortable as her gaze rested especially on him. "Some of them," she went on, "might easily be broken and I wouldn't for the world have anything happen to my presents."

"We'll be careful," Bert promised for all the Bobbseys.

They set to work with eagerness. Shouts of surprise and pleasure came to them as the contents of the package were revealed. Most of them were beautiful, many of them useful.

"There's enough silver here for a hotel," said Nan as she gazed rapturously at a glittering collection of shining articles.

"And enough clocks for one in every room in the house," remarked Bert. "They'll have no excuse for not knowing the time. Freddie, look out!" he cried in a startled tone. "You'll drop that box!"

His warning came a little too late. Freddie, after making every effort to keep out of trouble, had let a carefully-wrapped package slip from his fingers. It fell to the floor with a thud! With the crash sank also the hearts of all the Bobbsey twins.

"Now you've done it," moaned Nan, "and after all that Miss Higgin said to us."

"You've got us in a pretty mess," growled Bert.

Freddie, almost in tears, looked from one to another with frightened eyes.

"I was sure I had hold of it all right," he quavered, "but it was heavier than I thought it was."

Nan was the first one to take a calmer view of the situation.

"Maybe it isn't broken, whatever it is," she said in a tone in which hope struggled with fear.

She picked up the box and shook it gently.

"Doesn't sound like broken glass or china," she said, her face brightening.

"Well, let's open the box and know the worst," observed Bert gloomily.

With quaking hearts and great care the children unwrapped the package. Great was their surprise to see a solid steel toasting rack!

Little giggles of relief broke from them as they viewed it.

"So much worry for nothing," sighed Nan.

From that time on they were as careful as possible. In a little while they reached the end of their task. After the gifts had been placed on a table the children set to work clearing up the wrappings. In doing so, Nan uttered an exclamation.

"Oh, my goodness!" she said. "Here's something we almost threw out! Look!" She held up the lid of a teapot. "It's so small we didn't notice it."

They soon found the pot to which the lid belonged. They had barely done so when Miss Higgin appeared.

"Oh, how prettily you have arranged my presents," she exclaimed, as she went from one to another of the charming gifts. "What would I have done without such splendid helpers? And not a thing broken!" she laughed.

On the way to the house the children met Miss Juliana. She said:

"I'm getting along splendidly with your dress, Nan. I'm sure you'll like it for it really is attractive looking. After I've finished it I'll have to complete some sewing which I'm doing for Hester. And after that I'll make you a new frock, Flossie, all full of ruffles and tiny frills. Wouldn't that be just what you'd like?"

"Oh, goody!" cried the little girl. "Do you mean the yellow one?"

The pleasant young lady nodded and smiled sweetly. As she was about to go on Bert asked suddenly:

"Miss Juliana, I wonder if you know that Hans Weser now is in Tuliptown."

The dressmaker stopped suddenly and looked very startled. She didn't say a word for a while but just stared thoughtfully into space. Finally she said:

"No, I didn't know that." She spoke very slowly, as if she were thinking of a lot of things in connection with Hans Weser. "If it's true that he is back, I am very sorry, for I had hoped never to see that man again."

Much later that same day when the Bobbseys were on their way home after the picnic Nan scolded Bert for having mentioned Hans Weser to Miss Juliana.

"I'm sorry now that I said anything," her twin admitted. "I spoke without thinking. But I wonder why she dislikes that Dutchman so?"

"I guess everybody does," said Flossie, pedaling her bicycle vigorously. "He must be an awful man."

As they neared Windmill Cottage they caught sight of Grandma Haarlem digging in the ground near the old mill.

"Still at it, poor old lady," remarked Bert. "I wonder if she will ever find the treasure."

"If there is one," sighed Nan.

"There *has* to be a treasure!" announced Freddie Bobbsey.

CHAPTER XIX

THE UNSEEN LISTENER

"I HOPE there is a treasure," said Nan with a sigh. "But maybe it's all in Grandma Haarlem's imagination, as Mother says."

"We did find a piece of gold the first day we got here. And it was real, too," Freddie reminded them.

"Yes, that was a funny thing," agreed Bert thoughtfully. "I felt sure that day there was a treasure, just as Grandma Haarlem said. But now I don't know what to think."

"Let's go 'round and help her dig," Freddie suggested. "Maybe she would like to rest a little while."

While Bert, Nan and Flossie went over to the mill, Freddie ran to the barn to get the spade which he had found at the Brown farm and had hidden for just this purpose. What was his surprise when he looked for it to discover that it had disappeared! He ran to the windmill as fast as his little legs would carry him.

"Bert, my spade's gone," he said breathlessly. "I left it in the barn and now it isn't there. What do you s'pose could have happened to it?"

"Maybe Emile took it," Bert suggested.

When the children asked Emile about it, the hired man said that he had not seen Freddie's spade, and that he had not known there was one in the barn. Then Bert made a startling statement. Suppose Herman Klaas, eager to continue the search for the buried treasure on his own account, had taken the shovel?

This suggestion opened the way for all sorts of wonderings. Would Klaas return to the farm some time in the night—perhaps that very night —to continue his digging?

Freddie brooded over this question most seriously. All by himself he came at last to a decision. He would be a real policeman! He would steal out when no one was looking and hide in the windmill. Then, if Klaas should come to look for the treasure, he, Freddie, would be on hand to catch him and hand him over to the authorities.

After dinner that evening Freddie stole away and put on his policeman's suit. He managed to get out of the house without attracting attention.

The mill looked very old and ghostly in the gathering darkness. The little boy's heart almost skipped a beat as he climbed the old steps and opened the sagging door. His uniform gave him courage, however. Policemen were never afraid of anything. And he was a policeman now, a real one! So he must be brave.

Sturdily the little boy climbed the stairs and made his way to the top of the windmill. There, amid the dust and cobwebs he sat down to wait for Klaas to come.

But Freddie was a very small boy. He had had an exciting day, had just eaten a hearty meal, and before he knew it his head was nodding and his eyes were closing in spite of himself.

He tried hard to fight off this drowsiness. He was sure policemen never get sleepy when they are on watch. And he was a real policeman. Still, he was most—awfully—sleepy—

How long he slept he didn't know. Suddenly he was awakened by somebody stumbling over an object at the foot of the mill. There was an exclamation and a voice growled:

"There are holes all around this place. I nearly broke my ankle that time!"

"Then you should look where you are going, Klaas," snapped a second voice.

Freddie was wide awake now. He had recognized both voices. One belonged to Herman Klaas. The other was that of Hans Weser!

Cautiously Freddie crept to the window and looked out. There, directly below him, were the dim shadows of two men. One of them struck a match to light a cigarette, but with an angry exclamation his companion struck the match from his hand.

"Be careful," he cried. "Do you want the people at the house to see a light here and come to find out who is searching for Grandma Haarlem's treasure? If there is one, which I doubt very much."

Klaas spoke up. "I've heard so much talk from different people around here about the old lady's grandson burying a lot of money before he went off to the war that I'm sure there's something to it. Then, too, his grandmother knows about it, else why should she keep on digging?"

"The woman is old. She has queer thoughts in her head," the Dutchman returned.

"I believe the grandson told her where he buried the money," Klaas persisted.

"Well, and if you are right, what is it you suggest we do?"

"That we try to find this treasure," said Klaas eagerly. "One man alone wouldn't have much chance, but two, working together—"

"And if we find it?" Weser broke in.

"Then we will be rich. You and I will go into

partnership. We will hire new attractions and get into the show business in a really big way. Come, what do you say?"

"Humph! We must first find the money," grunted Weser. "Well, I will try it with you, yes. But what is that noise?" he added in a startled voice. "People are coming this way. We must get out of here!"

Klaas dropped the spade he was holding. Before the two men could move, the beam of a flashlight carried by the older Bobbsey boy fell full on their faces. Behind him came Nan and Flossie. All three children looked very anxious and upset.

"Hello!" said Bert, stopping short at sight of the two men. "Have you seen anything of my little brother Freddie?"

"I'm here, Bert," said the small boy, appearing at the mill door. "I went up into the loft and then I fell asleep."

The Dutchman and Klaas exchanged startled glances. They looked at Freddie's uniform, which reminded them most uncomfortably of other uniforms worn by real policemen. Then they stared at Freddie, who was rubbing his eyes and blinking in the light of Bert's torch.

"You are sure you were asleep—all the time—yes?" said Weser's harsh voice. "You did not hear, by any chance, what myself and this good Klaas have been talking about?"

The two men seemed to hold their breaths while they waited for the little boy's answer. Freddie hesitated. He was confused by the sudden appearance of Bert and his sisters. Then, too, he was a little frightened by the manner of Hans Weser and Klaas.

He looked down at his policeman's uniform and the sight of it gave him courage. He straightened his small back and thrust out his chin.

"I heard what you said," he replied sturdily, "about Grandma Haarlem's treasure and how you were going to look for it yourselves. I guess," he quavered, "I guess I'd better arrest you in the name of the Law!"

Weser grew purple with rage. He took a step toward Freddie but Klaas caught the man's upraised arm.

"No use getting mad with a kid. Come along, Weser. Let's get out of here."

"You better not take my spade," said Freddie, "because I'm going to dig for Grandma Haarlem's treasure myself."

Klaas had stooped to pick up the shovel but changed his mind. He scowled at the "little policeman," left the spade lying where it was, and disappeared into the shadows with Weser.

"Come along, Freddie," said Nan, putting an arm about her small brother. "Mother has been terribly worried about you."

After recovering the shovel, the children trooped into the house. There Freddie was greeted by his mother with a mixture of scoldings and kisses. Then he was sent upstairs to bed.

It was no later than the next day that Bert happened to meet Weser while on an errand in town. To the lad's surprise the Dutchman stopped and acted as if he wanted to speak to the boy.

"I hear a great deal in Tuliptown about this monkey house of Ernest Brown," he said in what he tried to make a sincere tone. "It is a success, is it not? People come even from the neighboring towns to see it and they pay their good money. Is it not so?"

"Why yes," said Bert, on his guard. "Folks seem to like Mrs. Monkey, and no wonder. She's pretty smart, I can tell you."

"So! And Ernest Brown would not be sorry to get a little money, I suppose? If he would sell I would be willing to make him a good offer. Oh, yes, a very, very good offer."

"I'm sure he doesn't want to sell," said Bert in alarm. "Besides, he couldn't. The monkey doesn't belong to him."

The lad did not wait for further conversation

with the Dutchman, but pedaled back to Windmill Cottage as fast as his bicycle would take him. Once there, he went directly to his friend and warned him.

"Weser is up to something, Ernest. He wants to get hold of our show. Better watch out for him," he said.

So it came about that when the Dutchman approached Ernest later that same day on the matter of selling his show, the young man refused him at once. Going away in an ugly mood, Weser caught sight of Bert in the garden and shook his fist at the boy. Just one more score, apparently, that this unpleasant fellow felt he owed the Bobbsey family!

The next day had been set for the rehearsal of Miss Higgin's wedding at the church. The Bobbseys, Mrs. Van Doorn, and even Grandma Haarlem were to go.

At the time appointed the children started off in high spirits. Little did they realize what was going to happen at Windmill Cottage while they were away!

CHAPTER XX

THE WEDDING REHEARSAL

THE twins looked forward to the church rehearsal with great delight, for they felt it would be almost as beautiful as the real ceremony. Freddie was a little nervous, for he had forgotten to practise carrying the ring since he had been at Windmill Cottage. Suddenly he happened to think that nobody had told him what he was going to wear.

"P'raps I ought to wear my p'liceman's suit."

"Oh, no," laughed Mrs. Bobbsey. "There's no one to be arrested at a wedding ceremony. You leave it to me, young man, and I'll dress you up."

Then she showed him a surprise. She had bought him a very smart little page boy suit. He liked it all but the collar, which he said was too tight for summer time.

As they drove to the church Mrs. Bobbsey gave the younger twins a little motherly advice,

"Now, you mustn't get the least bit excited," she said as she caressed Flossie's golden head and drew Freddie to her. "You, Flossie, are to walk

167

up the aisle before the other members of the wedding party and try to keep in step with the music. Don't go too fast. Scatter some flowers for the bride to walk on, but don't use them up too fast or they'll be all gone before you reach the altar.

"And you, Freddie," she continued, "are to keep in time with the others. When you get to the altar, let the best man take the ring. And be careful not to drop it."

The children promised to keep all these things in mind. At the church they found a number of visitors, perhaps guests who could not come to the real wedding. The young twins decided they would have to do their best in front of all these people!

Nan, Bert, and their mother found seats in the center of the church, while Flossie and Freddie were asked to join the wedding group gathered in the vestry. The children were a bit shy and nervous, but it is doubtful whether they were more so than was their mother. From long experience she had found that all sorts of unexpected things might be looked for from her twins. Miss Higgin and Jack Benson, with the best man and bridesmaids, greeted the little Bobbseys warmly and soon put them at their ease.

From the choir loft of the church there soon

came the deep notes of the organ playing the beautiful wedding march. The groom and the best man hurried off to take their places in another part of the church. Then at a signal Flossie led the procession, scattering flowers as she walked up the aisle. She was followed by Freddie carrying a white satin pillow. The other members of the party entered the church in step to the music and proceeded up the aisle.

At the altar the minister stood waiting. Flossie forgot what her mother had told her, and scattered flowers so freely that her basket was almost empty when she was only halfway to the altar. For a moment panic seized her. She looked about her as though she thought of sliding into one of the pews and hiding her head.

But no, that would never do. What would the bride think? What would her mother say? No, she must not disgrace them. Although she was very close to tears, the little girl bravely took command of herself and moved on, throwing imaginary flowers with hands that tried hard not to tremble.

Freddie, too, had his troubles. When the time came in the ceremony for him to let the best man take the ring, the small boy's hands trembled so he let the ring slide off the pillow. It dropped to the floor. He had to slip down on his hands and knees to recover it. It was a very flushed face that appeared above his page boy collar when he finally found it and handed it to the best man, who had all he could do to hold back a smile.

"We had better sew the ring to the pillow," whispered Nan to her mother. Mrs. Bobbsey nodded.

The rest of the ceremony proceeded without further mishap, and once more the party moved down the aisle and into the vestry. Miss Higgin threw her arms about Flossie and hugged her.

"You dear child," she said as she kissed her. "You're too sweet to be true. You did splendidly."

"And that's true of you too, my lad," chimed in Jack Benson as he put his hand on Freddie's head. "Lots of boys would have got rattled had they dropped the ring and would have taken a long time in finding it. You got it back as quick as lightning."

The youngsters glowed under the praise. It took away, as it was intended to do, all the sad feelings in their little hearts because of the trifling errors they had made.

"Now we're going to my house for something to eat," said Miss Higgin.

At her home there were many kinds of good things. On these the twins feasted to their hearts' content.

"Wish there could be a wedding rehearsal every day," declared Bert with his mouth full of cake.

"Perhaps that would be going a little too far," laughed Jack Benson who overheard the remark.

But the rest of the Bobbsey Twins backed up Bert in what he said!

Grandma Haarlem had been one of those who had witnessed the rehearsal, but it is doubtful that she had given it her close attention. Her thoughts were far away. At luncheon she was still in a strange mood and kept talking to herself in a dreamy voice.

"It won't be long now," the children heard her murmur. "He'll be coming back. Then I won't have to do any more digging."

Nan turned to Bert. "She's thinking of her grandson," the girl whispered.

"Yes, poor old lady," replied her brother in the same low tone. He turned to his mother. "Do you think she has really lost her mind?" he asked softly.

"It's hard to tell," replied Mrs. Bobbsey sadly, "but my heart bleeds for the poor lonely old soul."

Miss Higgin came by at that moment and patted Flossie's golden head.

"You'll have a different kind of flower for

your basket at the real wedding," she said. "They'll be orange blossoms. They're going to be brought here by airplane from Florida."

"By airplane!" exclaimed Freddie. "Golly, I wish I could fly with them."

"You'd better come with us instead," laughed Nan. "Mother says it's time to go home. We've stayed longer than anybody else."

Mrs. Bobbsey drove the car back to Windmill Cottage. When she and the children arrived there they found Ernest Brown standing near Mrs. Monkey's house, his hand resting against it. He looked the picture of sadness.

"The monkey's gone!" said the young man.

"Gone!" the Bobbseys echoed.

Flossie looked into the little house. Everything was in order, but there was no cute Mrs. Monkey sitting on the couch or huddled up in the doll's bed. Flossie began to cry.

"I want Mrs. Monkey," she sobbed.

"I've looked everywhere," said Ernest unhappily. "I've even been up to the old mill. By the way," he added, "there's been some digging going on there recently. The ground's all spaded up in front of the mill!"

"Somebody has been looking for the treasure while we've been away," cried Nan.

"Golly, I hope he didn't find it!" said Freddie.

CHAPTER XXI

MRS. MONKEY DISAPPEARS

"Do you think the monkey ran away?" asked Bert.

"Perhaps I shouldn't say it," replied Ernest as the children looked at him, "but I have a feeling she may have been stolen."

Flossie nodded as tears came into her eyes.

"Mrs. Monkey was so tame she would never have gone away by herself," said the little girl.

"If she was stolen who could have done it?" wondered Nan aloud.

"Gee, how about Hans Weser?" Bert exclaimed suddenly. "He was keen to get the monkey, you know, Ernest. When you wouldn't sell her maybe he made up his mind to help himself."

"I feel sure Weser hasn't the nerve to do a thing like that," said Ernest thoughtfully. "Not that he would hesitate to steal, but he'd get some one else to do the work for him. He wouldn't take a chance himself."

"Some one else to do his work for him," Nan

repeated. She was thoughtful for a moment; then her face brightened as she said quickly, "How about Herman Klaas? Do you think he could have done it?"

"I wouldn't put it past him. But we can't prove anything," said Ernest sadly. "This looks like the end of the show, just when it was making such good money, too. Poor old Tony. I don't know how I am going to break the news to him."

The children all looked very downcast for a few minutes. Bert suddenly said:

"I'm going to try to find Klaas. I want to have a talk with him."

"Think he'd tell you if he had stolen the monkey?" asked Ernest with a grin. "Better leave Klaas alone, Bert. He may harm you."

However, the Bobbsey boy was determined to find Klaas and question him in the hope of learning what had become of Mrs. Monkey. Although he felt there was not much hope, the other children agreed with him that the plan was worth trying anyway.

They got on their bicycles, tired as they were, and pedaled off toward Tuliptown. They inquired of several persons along the road whether they had seen any one answering Klaas's description, but no one seemed to know anything about the fellow.

They were turning back, discouraged, when who should step out of the woods directly in their path but the man they were seeking!

"Hello!" exclaimed Klaas, evidently as much surprised as the children were. "Looking for somebody?"

"Yes, a little monkey," blurted Bert, staring straight at the man.

"If you had a mirror handy you might see one," remarked Klaas with a wicked grin.

Bert flushed but kept his temper.

"It's Ernest Brown's monkey I'm talking about," he said. "It got away from him somehow. He doesn't know whether it wandered off by itself or has been stolen by somebody. You haven't seen anything of it, have you?"

Klaas's brow darkened. "Are you hinting that I stole the monkey?" he fairly shouted.

"I'm not hinting anything," said Bert. "I'm just asking you what I'd ask anyone else, whether you have seen anything of the monkey."

"You can't smooth it over like that," snarled Klaas. "You used the word stole and you mean me. Why, you little whippersnapper, I've a good mind to give you a hiding. I could break you in two between my fingers just like—just like—"

He looked about him and his eyes fell on an iron spike. He picked it up.

"Like this," he said, and before the awe-struck gaze of the little group he bent the rod double with his two hands.

"Or like this," he went on, turning to a sapling near where he was standing.

With a mighty wrench he tore the young tree loose from its roots.

"You see," he said, "it doesn't do to make me mad. Why, I could throw one of you up into the top of a tree without half trying!"

He grabbed Flossie and swung her aloft as though he were about to carry out that purpose. The little girl cried with fright, and the rest of the Bobbseys jumped on the man like so many wildcats, Bert using his fists and Nan and Freddie clawing wildly at the fellow's big arms.

So sudden was the attack that Klaas staggered back in surprise. Then he lowered Flossie rather shamefacedly to the ground.

"Of course, I was only fooling," he said sheepishly. "I wouldn't hurt the little girl for anything. That was only to teach you that it's a bad thing to get me mad."

He strode off without another word while the indignant children dried their little sister's tears.

"The big brute!" exclaimed Nan, her eyes flashing.

"Brute is the name for him," said Bert, "but

you can see that he's ashamed of himself. I suppose I shouldn't have used the word 'stole' when I didn't have any real proof at all that Klaas had taken the monkey."

Flossie soon recovered her usual good spirits and the search for the missing animal went on. It resulted in nothing, so a rather sad group of Bobbseys returned to announce their lack of success to Ernest. He, too, had been hunting desperately, combing the town and the surrounding countryside without discovering any trace of the missing pet.

"This is the end of the show," he said hopelessly. "Just when it was going so nicely, too. But I'm not thinking only of myself. There's old Tony in the hospital. It will break his heart when he learns that his pet is missing. Why, the monkey is all he has to depend on for a living. I can't bear the idea of breaking the bad news to him."

"I tell you what," volunteered Bert. "You leave that to Nan and me. It will be a hard job and I hate doing it, but it will give you more time to go on looking. Is that all right, Nan?" he asked his sister.

"Surely," returned his twin promptly. "I wish it were better news but somebody will have to tell him."

"That's mighty good of you both," said Ernest

gratefully. "As you say, that will give me more time to hunt. Break it to the old man as gently as you can."

"We'll do it the first thing in the morning," they promised.

As early as possible the next day they set off. Freddie and Flossie went along. They soon arrived at the hospital, a beautiful, up-to-date building with spacious grounds surrounding it. On the lawn under some trees Nan and Bert left the little twins to await their return while they themselves entered the hospital.

There they were pleasantly received. When the children stated their errand, a white-clad nurse led the way to the old Italian's room.

"Some visitors to see you, Tony," she said, ushering them in. She left them with the warning to stay no longer than a quarter of an hour. They found the old man lying comfortably between snow-white sheets. An equally white pillow under his head contrasted strongly with his dark complexion and showed up the lines in his face.

Yet he was pleasant looking. His twinkling black eyes lighted up as they rested on the two young folks.

"Ze pretty girl an' ze fine boy come to see ole Tony," he said as he extended a seamed and toil-worn hand in greeting. "Eet is good for zem to come. Dere ees so few fren's that Tony has dese days. You come bring bright sunshine to Tony."

The children acknowledged his greeting warmly, but at the same time their hearts sank as they thought of the cloud that would come over Tony when he should hear the news they had to bring.

"We are friends of Ernest Brown," said Bert. "You know, the young man who has been exhibiting your monkey while you have been here ill."

"Oh, dat Ernest," exclaimed Tony, a broad smile coming over his face. "He one fine young man! He showa de monk while Tony ees seeck an' he make much money for Tony. Look," and he swept his hand proudly over the room. "All da fine things, da white sheets, da sof' pillas an flowers on da stand. All dees come from da money Ernest maka wid da monk. He good boy, dat Ernest."

"He sure is," agreed Bert.

The boy looked at Nan. How, he wondered, could they bear to tell this simple old fellow the sad news that would wipe away all smiles from his face? Bert motioned to Nan to do the speaking. She motioned back to him. Neither of them could say a word.

While they were trying desperately to bring themselves to the point of breaking the bad news, Freddie and Flossie were seated on a bench in the park-like enclosure in front of the hospital, calmly munching peanuts. As they sat under the shade of a great tree, Freddie, glancing carelessly upward, gave a startled exclamation.

"Look, Flossie, look!" he cried.

Flossie raised her eyes. There, peering through the branches above them, was the monkey!

CHAPTER XXII

CAPTURING THE RUNAWAY

FLOSSIE's eyes sparkled as her glance fell on the little animal. She started up from the bench but Freddie pulled her back.

"Sh-h!" he whispered. "If you jump around you'll scare him. P'raps we can coax him down."

It was hard for Flossie to control her excitement, but she did so as well as she could while Freddie took a handful of peanuts and held them up for the monkey to see.

It was a tempting bait and Mrs. Monkey soon showed signs of yielding. Yet it took her a long time to make up her mind. The little taste of liberty she had had was sweet, and she seemed in no hurry to return to captivity.

Yet she was very hungry, for she hadn't had a real meal since noon of the previous day. Carefully, and very slowly did she come down from one branch to another until she was on the lowest bough.

"Here she is!" whispered Flossie. "Hold the peanuts up high."

Freddie did so and the sight was too much for Mrs. Monkey to resist. Still she wanted to get the peanuts, yet keep her liberty too. So she swung her tail over the lowest branch and hung by it while she swayed to and fro and reached out a paw for the nuts.

"Isn't she cute?" whispered Flossie with a giggle.

"She isn't as smart as she thinks she is, though," said Freddie. "She isn't going to get these nuts until she comes down from that tree."

He held up the food just out of reach of the little animal's paw. Again and again the monkey tried to get it, but the little boy was on his guard and kept them from being snatched.

For some minutes this went on. Finally the monkey gave up. Her freedom was sweet, but the nuts looked mighty good! She swung herself up again to the branch, then climbed to the ground, and sidled over to the pair.

Freddie reached down and grabbed her with one arm while with his remaining free hand he thrust a nut into her mouth. Then she surrendered. She sat in his arms, eagerly munching, while Flossie patted her shaggy coat and shook her by the hand.

"How do you do, Mrs. Monkey?" she said gravely.

"Got her at last," exclaimed Freddie exultingly. "Wasn't it lucky that we just happened to sit down under this tree?"

"And won't Ernest be glad!" said Flossie. "He felt so bad about losing her."

"And think what Bert and Nan will say when they find we caught the monkey all by ourselves," said Freddie proudly.

"We'll go and tell them right away," suggested Flossie.

"Yes, but let Mrs. Monkey finish the nuts first," replied Freddie. "Golly, how she's eating them She must have been awful hungry."

They waited impatiently until the little creature had made a clean sweep of the nuts. Then they rose from their seats and made their way to the main entrance of the hospital.

While all this was going on, Nan and Bert had been having a hard time keeping the talk going with Tony. They knew that they had to tell him about the loss of his monkey. That was what they had come for, what they had promised Ernest they would do, and they couldn't leave the hospital without carrying it out.

The old Italian was so happy, so content in his surroundings, so confident that everything was go ing well with him. The children still hesitated to destroy all his joy by giving him the news they had come to bring.

Still, it had to be done. Which one of them should do it? They looked at each other with that question in their eyes. At last in desperation Bert cleared his throat.

"I'm sorry to tell you, Tony——" he began.

Just then there was a racket out in the hall. They could hear excited cries, voices of nurses, the deeper tones of doctors, and the shrill notes of children.

"What's the matter, I wonder?" exclaimed Nan, rising to her feet and hurrying to the door. She swung it open. "Why, it's Flossie and Freddie," she cried, as she heard the voices of her sister and brother. "What have they come in here for? I thought they were to stay in the park."

"So they were," replied Bert. "I suppose they got tired of waiting."

Just then a little procession came in view. It consisted of a couple of nurses, one of the internes, and Flossie and Freddie trudging in the rear, the latter holding tightly to the monkey in his arms.

"Oh, they have Mrs. Monkey!" cried Nan in delight.

"You don't mean it!" exclaimed Bert with a feeling of immense relief.

"Here she is," declared Freddie proudly as he came into the room. "They weren't going to let us in the hospital at first, but when we told them she belonged to Tony it was all right."

"Yes," put in one of the nurses with a smile. "It isn't very often that we let monkeys into the hospital, but the kiddies begged so hard that we thought we'd make an exception this time. Besides, we thought it might be a good thing for Tony to see an old friend."

She was right about that. The sight of the little creature put Tony in a state of delight. He grasped his pet and hugged her, murmuring to her, smoothing her coat, and fairly devouring her with his eyes.

"She come back to ole Tony," he cried with tears of joy in his eyes. "Oh, eet ees good. She love old Tony. She come to see him. Oh, eet ees good."

The children looked on happily at the reunion of the old man with his pet. The nurses, too, were touched by what they saw.

Then the whole story came out. No longer were Nan and Bert tongue-tied. The words fairly tumbled over one another as they told of the long search for the little creature.

And Flossie and Freddie, you may be sure, were not far behind in telling about the final capture. Tony thanked them again and again, and the joy in the old man's eyes was pay aplenty for what they had done.

They chattered for a while. Then, mindful of the nurse's warning, Bert took the monkey in his arms. Promising to keep Tony fully informed of the doings of his pet, the children left the room.

As they were going down the corridor the same nurse stopped them and asked them to go for a few minutes into the children's ward so that the youngsters there might have a glimpse of Mrs. Monkey and her cunning ways. The little tots there went wild with delight as the pet, comforted by the peanuts and soothed by the visit to old Tony, went through all her tricks. The Bobbsey Twins were equally overjoyed in acting as showmen.

The happiness of Ernest Brown when the monkey was restored to him was beyond all words. "I can't thank you enough," he said heartily as he placed the little runaway in the glass house. "I've been pretty worried, I can tell you. Never felt worse in my life. Now everything is fine. I'm glad, too, that if the monkey had to go wandering that way she did so of her own accord. If Weser or Klaas had stolen her there's no knowing how roughly they might have treated her."

Mrs. Monkey herself seemed glad enough to get back into her old quarters. After all, there is no place like home. There at least one can feel sure of regular meals.

"No more of your tricks, old lady, except the ones we teach you," warned Ernest, as he patted her head. "I'll keep a closer watch on you than I did before and if you get away from me again you're smarter than I think you are."

The monkey gave a little squeal which might have been taken as a promise to be good in the future. It had been a long morning for the Bobbsey twins, filled with exciting adventure. At the mid-day meal they did full justice to the appetizing lunch placed before them, telling their mother as well as they could, while they ate, all that had happened.

Mrs. Bobbsey listened with interest and shared their delight in the recapture of the monkey. A graver expression came into her face, however, when she heard of the time they had had with Klaas.

"He's a dangerous man with that temper of his and his great strength," she said. "I want you children to have nothing to do with him. I only wish that he were out of the neighborhood. And I feel the same way about Hans Weser. Tuliptown would be a better place with both of them out of it."

Later on in the day the children caught sight of

Grandma Haarlem wearily bending over a spade in the vicinity of the old mill.

"Still looking for the treasure," remarked Nan with a sigh. "Poor old lady!"

"And always will be at it until she drops," prophesied Bert. "I wish some fairy would come along with a magic wand, just wave it over the place and show the old lady the treasure. But probably there's nothing there to show."

"Nothing, I'm afraid, but what may have come to her in dreams," agreed Nan sadly.

"Golly, I wish I could help her," put in Freddie.

"So do I," echoed Flossie.

Bert looked about him. His eyes fell on a big rock only a short distance from the door of the mill. A thought struck him.

"I've heard sometimes of treasure being hidden in holes under big stones," he said.

Instantly the children were on fire with excitement.

"Golly, I never thought of that!" said Freddie. "Let's go!"

CHAPTER XXIII

A THRILLING HUNT

"THERE are lots of things you never thought of," said Bert to Freddie with the calm superiority of an elder brother.

"Anyway, I found Mrs. Monkey and you didn't," Freddie came back at him.

"I helped find her," put in Flossie, not to be cheated out of her share of the glory.

"That was just luck," teased Bert. "But now about this rock—"

"You don't really think the treasure might be under it, do you, Bert?" asked Nan breathlessly.

"It may be if there is a treasure," returned her twin. "Anyway, I'm going to have a look."

"Wouldn't it be wonderful if we should find it?" exclaimed Nan. "Just think of being able to hand the treasure to poor Grandma Haarlem! But how are we going to move the rock, Bert? It's a pretty big one."

It was big indeed and Bert eyed it dubiously.

He pushed against it with all his might and fancied he could detect a very slight movement.

"I thought I felt it move a bit," he said. "It doesn't seem to be very deep in the ground. Here, let all of us get together and see if we can push it away."

The children went at it with a will, and under their united efforts they could feel the huge stone move. Yet they knew they could not get it out of its place without additional help.

"I'll tell you what we'll do," said Bert as they paused a while. "Freddie, you go and get your spade and we'll dig all around the rock so as to loosen the earth that's holding it. That'll be the first thing. I've noticed in the barn a long iron lever such as railroad men use when they're prying up a track. Maybe that will help us out."

Freddie was off like a flash while Bert went to the barn and found the long steel rod that he had remembered seeing there. He and Nan set to work digging around the stone, each taking a turn when the other grew tired. After a long time, during which they had expended a good deal of effort, they had dug all about the rock and revealed the lower part.

"There, that ought to make the rest easy," said Bert as he laid aside the spade and grasped the heavy lever. "Now I'll lay this under the bottom of the rock and when I count three we'll all pull down on the long end of the rod. If that doesn't bring it nothing will."

They grasped the rod tightly.

"Ready?" asked Bert. "One-two—*three*!"

At the word "three" the children bore down on the lever with all their strength.

"Almost got it that time," shouted Bert. "Now, once more!"

This time they were rewarded, for the big stone finally yielded and rolled down the slight slope on which it had been standing.

"Hooray!" cried Bert as they all dropped the rod and stood panting for breath.

Everyone gleefully crowded around the spot where the rock had stood.

"There isn't any hole," exclaimed Freddie in disappointment as he saw no sign of a cavity.

"That doesn't mean anything," declared Bert stoutly. "If anyone put a treasure there, he wouldn't have left it right against the rock itself. He'd have dug down beneath it and that's what we're going to do."

He seized the spade and set to work, Nan taking her turn in relieving him. They dug and dug until they had reached a depth of nearly two feet. Then the spade rang against a shelf of solid rock.

The twins looked at one another in dismay.

They had been following a false clue. All their work had been for nothing!

"The same luck as Grandma Haarlem has had," murmured Nan disconsolately.

"Too bad," said Bert. "All that effort and no reward."

"Well, after all, it hasn't been such a bad day," said Nan, brightening. "We haven't found the treasure but we did find the monkey. That made old Tony very happy."

Whatever disappointment they felt about the treasure was soon forgotten in the excitement that filled the cottage. Much was going on in preparation for Miss Higgin's wedding. When the actual day for the ceremony arrived, every one was on tiptoe with happy anticipation.

Mr. Bobbsey was to be on hand, and all the children ran out to welcome him as he stepped from his car. They greeted him with the delight they always felt at sight of him, and he was equally happy as he hugged and kissed them all, hoisting Flossie, his "little fat fairy," to his shoulder.

"All of you are brown as Indians," he chuckled as he led the little procession into the house. "I can see that Tuliptown's doing you a lot of good."

The rehearsal for the wedding had been exciting enough for the children, but was as nothing compared to that of the day of the wedding. The

children were up early and stirring around. There
was a great fuss about Bert and Nan's gifts,
which seemed to get themselves mislaid out of
sheer contrariness. Finally Mrs. Van Doorn put
them on the piano and stood guard over them herself.

"So! If they get away now they will have to
walk over me," said the good woman. The twins
chuckled at the thought of the wedding presents
walking over Mrs. Van Doorn.

All was in readiness at last and Daddy Bobbsey
drove his family over to the Higgin house. Bridesmaids were already beginning to arrive, flowers
were massed everywhere, and the air was festive
with the sound of voices and laughter.

Amid the gay scene there was one note of anxiety,
however. The orange blossoms which were to have
been brought from Florida by plane for the bride
had not arrived, and the party was in something
of a flutter.

"I don't know what can be keeping that aviator,"
said Mrs. Higgin nervously. "If he doesn't arrive
in time Hester will be terribly disappointed."

At this moment Mrs. Higgin caught sight of the
Bobbsey children. She greeted them cordially, and
noticing the carefully wrapped packages which
Bert and Nan still carried, called out:

"More wedding presents for Hester? Why, how

nice of you children to think of her. I'll take them
to her at once."

"What will you take to me?" asked a sweet
voice. The bride herself, very lovely in her satin
gown and flowing veil, was standing in the doorway.

"Just a couple of little presents Bert and I made
for you," said Nan, suddenly shy. "We saved them
until today to surprise you."

"Oh, how nice! And you say you made them?
Come here, everybody," she cried to the other
members of the wedding party, "and see what I
have. More presents!"

They all gathered around to watch the bride
open Nan's package. She took out the dainty apron
with the pretty Dutch scene in the corner which
the Bobbsey girl had embroidered so carefully.

"How lovely! And what dainty, fine stitches
you have put in it, Nan. Oh, thank you so much."
She kissed Nan in appreciation. Bert looked a little
uncomfortable for fear she might do the same to
him.

"And what's this?" she added, picking up the
boy's gift. "It looks big and feels heavy. Do you
think I could guess what it is through the paper
wrapping, Bert?"

"I'm afraid not. It isn't very much," stammered
the lad, trying not to look as embarrassed as he

felt. "I thought you might put it around some place in your new house. I—I hope it works."

"Why, it's a windmill." The tissue paper and ribbon slipped from Miss Higgin's fingers as she held Bert's present so that everyone could see it. "It looks just like the one at Windmill Cottage."

"It's a weather vane, really," Bert explained. "Some day when you have time I'll show you how it works."

"I'll hold you to that promise," said Miss Higgin gaily. "Listen! Is that an airplane I hear?" she added, running to the window.

Others had heard the low, throbbing drone of an airplane motor. They flocked excitely to the windows, searching the sky with eager eyes.

"There it is!" shouted Freddie, whose sharp eyes had been the first to spot the tiny speck in the sky.

"Let's go out and see it land," cried Bert, and dashed out into the open, followed by Nan and the little twins.

"Golly, he's going to come down right in the field," cried Freddie.

The children ran to a fence that surrounded the open territory. Some of the older folks stopped them for fear they might get in the way of the descending machine, and also to keep them from getting dirty! Down came the big man-made bird, spiraling gracefully toward the field. It struck the ground lightly and ran for a hundred yards or so before the pilot brought it to a stop.

A man equipped with flying helmet, gloves and goggles climbed out. Then from the fuselage he drew a large package and made his way toward the house.

Everyone made room for him, the children gazing with eager interest at the birdman who had come down from the skies.

The aviator found a warm welcome at the house. Mrs. Higgin took the flowers from him, thanking him for all the trouble he had gone to in order to deliver them in time.

"You must come to the ceremony with us," said the good woman warmly. "Afterward we want you to have coffee and sandwiches before you begin your long trip back. Now please don't refuse," she added as the newcomer seemed about to protest. "The bride asks particularly that you be present to see her married, and that you come back later for a piece of her wedding cake."

"Well, in that case I can't refuse," said the pilot with an attractive smile.

While the bridesmaids opened the package that had come all the way from Florida and exclaimed over the orange blossoms, fresh and dewy on their bed of damp moss, the aviator settled himself on a garden bench just outside the door. He evidently was well pleased with the successful performance of his mission.

He was a tall man, wiry and muscular, and had a frank, open face. Bert, who lingered behind the others in the hope of having a word with the pilot, thought he noticed something familiar about the man. He wondered if he might have seen him somewhere before.

The boy had little time to think about the matter, however, for the wedding party now was ready to start for the church. He and the other members of his family went along with them.

Bert and Nan, together with their mother and father, were seated in a part of the church where they had a full view of Grandma Haarlem. The aviator, whose name was Harper, sat in a pew on the opposite side.

The old lady, dressed in a quaint but very attractive Dutch costume, was paying little attention to the wedding ceremony. She appeared as if in a dream, her lips moving slightly.

"As though she were seeing visions," whispered Nan in her brother's ear.

"More likely thinking of the treasure," said Bert. "But look! Her eyes are open wide enough now. See how she's staring at that pilot!"

CHAPTER XXIV

THE AVIATOR

THERE was a look of more than ordinary interest in Grandma Haarlem's eyes as she stared at the aviator. Nan and Bert saw her lean forward in her pew to get a better look at the man's face. Her forehead was drawn into a deep frown, and the hands that gripped the head of her cane were taut and strained.

Puzzled, the children looked again at Mr. Harper. He sat very straight and stiff in his seat, looking like a normal, good-natured fellow who had been caught in a rather unusual situation and was a trifle self-conscious about it. However, there was nothing strange about him as far as the children could see. Why should Grandma Haarlem be looking at him the way she was?

"I wonder what she sees in him that interests her so?" Nan whispered.

Bert said nothing, but a staggering, impossible

suspicion had flashed across his mind. He realized now why the young aviator's face had seemed familiar to him!

"I'm beginning to imagine things just the way Grandma Haarlem does," he told himself. "It can't be so!"

There was no chance for further conversation between Nan and Bert. The wedding party had reached the altar, the bridesmaids and ushers had stepped aside, and the bride and groom were standing before the minister. Nan could see just the top of Flossie's fair head as she stood with the flower basket over her arm, looking like a little flower herself in her lovely dress.

When the beautiful words of the marriage ceremony began, everyone was very quiet as he listened to the responses of the bride and groom. Nan saw Mrs. Higgin touch her eyes with her handkerchief when the bride said "I do." Mr. Higgin, who had given his daughter away, took off his glasses and wiped them very carefully before restoring them to their proper place on his nose.

Freddie looked very cute and boyish as he held the pillow for the best man to take the ring and give it to the groom. Nan and Bert exchanged understanding glances, for they knew just how relieved their little brother must feel to have done so without dropping it!

At last the lovely ceremony was over. Nan and Bert found themselves hustled into a car with several other guests and whisked off to the Higgins' house for the reception.

The little twins were beaming. Everyone made a great fuss over them, complimenting them on the successful parts they had taken in the wedding ceremony.

The bride came over and kissed Freddie, Flossie and Nan, and held out her hand to Bert. She looked very happy.

"I hate to part with you, you've been such darlings," she said. "But you will come to see us just as soon as we get back from our wedding trip, won't you? And Freddie, *you didn't drop the ring* !"

Then she was gone in a swirl of white satin and orange blossoms. Freddie swelled out his little chest until it looked as if he would burst the seams in his jacket.

"I didn't fall in the wedding cake, either!" he pronounced, remembering Hans Weser's cruel prophecy.

"Don't boast. There's still time," teased Bert. Then he grinned to show Freddie he really didn't mean it.

While the children were enjoying their refreshments, Grandma Haarlem came over toward them.

making her way slowly through the groups of wedding guests. The old lady seemed to be laboring under intense excitement. Her hand trembled on her cane and her cheeks looked flushed and feverish.

"Do you know where that young man is, the one who calls himself Harper?" she demanded. "Is he still here? Oh, tell me quickly, quickly!"

"I heard someone say he was going over to the airport from here," Bert said, looking in surprise at the old lady.

"I think I heard his plane take off a minute ago," Nan added.

Grandma Haarlem wrung her hands desperately. There were tears in her eyes.

"I must see him! I have to talk to him!" she cried. "Oh, he must not get away until I have spoken to him again! Oh, will no one help an old lady? Will no one go after him and bring him back?"

Some of the guests, among whom were Mr. and Mrs. Bobbsey, had been impressed by the desperate appeal. Mr. Bobbsey stepped forward and took Grandma Haarlem's shaking hand in his.

"My car is right outside. I'll get to the airfield as fast as I can," he said. "If young Harper has not yet started on his trip south I'll bring him back to you, I promise."

"Oh, bless you, bless you," said the old lady brokenly. "And hurry, please!"

As Mr. Bobbsey rushed out to his car the twins were right behind him.

"Daddy, may we come?" they asked breathlessly.

"Yes, yes, hop in. Only be quick!"

Then they were off, roaring down the road. It would be nip and tuck, Mr. Bobbsey knew, should they be able to catch the aviator at the airfield; but if the thing were possible, he was determined to accomplish it for Grandma Haarlem's sake. He pressed his foot down on the accelerator.

It was fortunate for the Bobbsey family that they met no traffic officers on that wild dash. Freddie was the only policeman they saw the whole way, and he definitely was in full approval of what they were doing.

With a grinding of brakes they drew up outside the airfield. A big plane, which they recognized as the one belonging to Harper, was at the far end of the field ready for a take-off. As Daddy Bobbsey and the twins tumbled breathlessly from their car they saw the propeller begin to revolve. Toward the gates they dashed and past a policeman, who tried in vain to stop them. Then they ran out onto the field.

"Stop that plane!" Mr. Bobbsey cried to a hand-

ful of startled officials who turned toward him
and the younger Bobbseys. "Don't let the pilot get
away! Hold him!"

"It's a matter of life and death," shouted Freddie, who had heard the phrase somewhere and
thought it a very good one to use now.

A mechanic ran toward the machine, waving his
arms. The pilot evidently saw him, for the plane,
already in motion, came to a stop within a few
feet of the fellow.

The pilot, fumbling with the straps of his helmet, climbed to the ground. When he turned toward them the children were overjoyed to see that
he was their man, the aviator, Mr. Harper.

"What's the idea?" he grumbled to the mechanic who had stopped him. "Got a leak in my
gas tank or something?"

The man only grinned and waved a hand toward
Daddy Bobbsey and the twins, who by this time
had come up to the plane.

"Folks to see you," he explained. "Seems to be
something very important."

The young man's face brightened as he recognized the Bobbsey family. His smile included them
all.

"Something I can do for you, sir?" he asked of
Mr. Bobbsey.

"It's Grandma Haarlem," said Flossie breathlessly. "She wants to see you. She said to bring you back—"

"Dead or alive!" finished Freddie so importantly that everybody laughed, including the aviator.

"Hardly that," said Mr. Bobbsey, putting a hand on his young son's head. "But we did promise the old lady, who seemed in a state of extreme agitation, to persuade you to come back to the Higgin house with us."

"She wants to see you very badly," Nan added.

"But why?" returned the aviator, puzzled. "I don't know her, do I? What did you say her name is?"

"Haarlem." It was Bert who answered. Now he added, remembering how he had been struck by the resemblance while in church, "You look a lot like her, even if she is so old. I noticed it at the wedding."

"Haarlem," repeated the young man in a bewildered way. "The name sounds familiar, yet I can't remember where I have heard it before. Haarlem—Haarlem—"

He broke off and looked at the children quickly. There was a mounting excitement in his voice as he added, "Tell me more about this old lady, please. You say she seemed to recognize me? And what is her full name?"

For a moment the children were non-plussed. They could not remember having heard her called anything but Grandma Haarlem. Suddenly Nan exclaimed:

"I believe I know what her first name is. Mrs. Van Doorn told me once and I remember now how pretty I thought it was. Elisabeta—that's what it is. Elisabeta Haarlem."

"Do you recognize it, Harper?" asked Mr. Bobbsey, watching the aviator's face.

"I begin to think I do, though I am not sure," said the young man with mounting excitement. "But I must see this old lady. I'll go back with you to the Higgin house and on the way you may tell me more about her if you will."

Leaving a mechanic to guard his plane, Harper went with the Bobbseys to the parked automobile. He acted like some one in a dream, both excited and bewildered.

On the way back, the twins told Mr. Harper all they knew about Grandma Haarlem; how for years she had mourned her grandson, presumably killed in the World War; how she believed that before leaving for France he had buried a fortune in gold and other valuables in or about the old mill on the Windmill Cottage grounds; how the poor old lady had looked for this treasure in vain over the years and would not give up the search even now when she was old and feeble and barely able to hobble about.

"She won't stop, poor old lady," Bert finished. "She still goes out with her spade and digs around the mill, although she never finds anything."

"Except one gold piece, and I found it," said Freddie proudly.

Harper came out of his strange dream to murmur thoughtfully:

"You say her name is Elisabeta, Elisabeta Haarlem. I should remember it, and I feel I do. But I can't—"

He broke off and put his hands to his head in a desperate gesture. Then he sank back against the cushions with a sigh of weariness.

"I can't remember," he muttered. "I just can't remember."

When they reached the Higgin house Mr. Bobbsey went in first to prepare Grandma Haarlem for the return of the pilot. The children followed with Harper.

When the old lady saw him she gave a queer little choking gasp and hobbled forward with her arms outstretched.

"You *are* my grandson," she cried. "My dear, dear boy!"

CHAPTER XXV

FOUND AT LAST

THE children felt tears spring to their eyes as the young man caught Grandma Haarlem in his arms and carried her over to a couch. He placed her very gently among the pillows and knelt down beside her.

"Grandmother!" he said, catching the old woman's fluttering hands in a strong grip. "I know you now. Everything has come back to me."

"You have been away so many, many years, Frederick," sighed the old lady. "I waited and waited after the war and when no word came to me of you I thought you must be dead. And I have needed you so. Why did you never come home?"

The man's face clouded. He released the hands he held and stood up, thrusting his own deep into his pockets.

"I have been sick, Grandmother," he explained, striding about and apparently not noticing the interested, sympathetic faces of the Bobbseys and the other wedding guests. "Not in my body, you understand, but in my mind. A shrapnel bullet caught me right here," he put a hand to the back of his head. "It was toward the end of the war, too, and up to that time I had come through almost without a scratch."

He paused and took his grandmother's hand in his own again.

"For a long time the doctors thought I was going to die, I guess. They said afterward in the hospital that I raved for days and nights and nearly set everybody crazy.

"I have no recollection of any of that, of course. But when I came to myself I had lost my identity. I couldn't remember who I was. My mind was a blank concerning everything that had happened to me up to that time. I knew only what people told me."

"You——you even forgot your name?" quavered the old lady.

"Yes, even that. I had a misty impression that it began with H so I took the name of Harper."

"And it is Haarlem, of course; Frederick Haarlem after my dear son, your father," said the old lady. She looked up at the tall man and an expression of supreme content came over her face. "Frederick, I want to go home. Will you take me with you, Grandson?"

There was great rejoicing at Windmill Cottage that night. Mrs. Van Doorn got up a gala dinner in honor of the occasion. Grandma Haarlem, her face all smiles, was seated as guest-of-honor at the head of the table. The aviator Harper, or Haarlem, as we now must call him, sat next to his grandmother, showing by a hundred little attentive acts how overjoyed he was to have found his aged relative.

"It's certainly good to be home again," he said, smiling around at the circle of happy, interested faces. "I feel like a man who has been exiled from his country for a long time and suddenly finds himself within sight of familiar shores."

Grandma Haarlem smiled and patted her grandson's hand.

"You won't go away again, Frederick? Not for a long time?" she begged.

"Well, I have my job with the Airways Company to think of, Grandmother. I can't afford to lose it in these times."

"You speak like a poor man, Frederick," said the old lady, leaning toward him with a puzzled frown. "But you are not poor. Have you forgotten the treasure?"

The children looked up eagerly, and even Mother and Daddy Bobbsey forgot to eat as they waited for the young man's answer. Here, at last, was the big test. Now they would know if Grandma Haarlem's tale of buried wealth had any foundation in fact!

Frederick Haarlem returned his grandmother's gaze with a frown as puzzled as her own.

"Treasure?" he returned. "What treasure?"

The children scarcely dared breathe while they waited for the old lady's answer. Flossie's eyes seemed ready to pop out of her head while Freddie held with both hands to his chair as if to restrain himself from jumping up out of it. Even the kitchen maid stopped still in the doorway to listen.

"Why, the treasure you buried before you went away to war." The old lady's face was flushed, her tone impatient. "Surely you must remember about it, Frederick."

The young man stared at her for several seconds. He seemed to be searching in his memory, painfully groping backward through the years. Suddenly his eyes brightened.

"Of course I remember!" he cried. "I recall fearing the bank would fail, so I took out my money and securities and buried them near— near—"

"Yes?" prompted the twins, while Grandma Haarlem leaned forward eagerly.

"Where did you bury the treasure, Grandson?" the old lady demanded.

The aviator's face clouded and he shook his head regretfully.

"Didn't you hide it up near the old mill?" Flossie prompted. "Grandma Haarlem said you did."

"That's what you said, Frederick. You told me where at the time, too, but it is so long ago that I have forgotten."

"I'm afraid I have, too, Grandma," the man confessed sadly. "My mind seems to be a complete blank as far as the treasure is concerned."

"I tell you what. Let's all go out to the old mill and dig," Freddie proposed. "I'll get my shovel!" The little boy scrambled down from the table, then stopped short to say politely, "Excuse me, please."

"May we, Mother?" asked Nan eagerly.

"If Mr. Haarlem wants to and if there are spades enough to go round," Mrs. Bobbsey consented. "While you're doing that I'll go up and pack. We have to leave this lovely place tomorrow or the next day."

"Golly, I hope we won't have to go before we find the treasure!" said Freddie.

However, it looked for a time as though that were just what they would have to do. Although all the spades and shovels about the place were put into action and Freddie, acting as the policeman, kept everyone busily working, no sign of a treasure could they find.

Frederick Haarlem had made some torch flares and planted them at various points about the mill to light the children at their work. For a while he helped them. Grandma Haarlem, with Dykie on her lap, sat on the edge of the group watching.

After some time the old lady complained of feeling cold, so her grandson picked her up in his arms and carried her to the house. Dykie remained with the children, sitting on the edge of the lighted space, dozing and blinking at the flares.

Several times the children grew weary and would have given up the search, had not Freddie kept them at it. Once he even arrested Flossie and would not give her her freedom until she promised to be good and go ahead with the digging.

They were all getting very tired, however, even the policeman, when Dykie, chasing a mouse into the mill, gave an entirely new turn to events. As she rushed across the clearing, the cat brushed against one of the torches and knocked it over so that the lighted end rested against the mill. In a moment the old wood flared up!

"Quick, throw dirt on that blaze!" cried Bert, rushing forward with a spadeful of loose earth. "All of you together now. Hurry, or the whole mill will go up in smoke!"

Nan, Freddie and Flossie rushed to Bert's side and began to shovel for all they were worth. A small section of the wall had fallen in and was blazing on the floor of the mill. Upon this the children piled the soft moist earth, smothering the flames.

It was a stubborn fire. Conquered in one place, it broke out in another, red fingers of flame running across the dry floor. The children persisted in fighting it, and after a long while, together with much digging, they finally put it out.

Panting and weary, Flossie, who was standing near one of the holes they had just made close to the wall of the mill, called to them. "Nan, Bert, Freddie, come over here," cried the little girl excitedly. "There's something in this hole!"

The others ran over to her. Bert, taking out his flashlight, directed its beam into the hole. Then he looked at the eager faces of the other children and whistled softly.

"An iron box!" he said. "Hurry, somebody, and give me a spade! We'll soon have this out!"

The children dug away in a frenzy of excitement. It is to be feared that Freddie and Flossie put more dirt into the hole than they got out. Finally the box was clear, and Bert and Freddie between them hauled it to the surface.

"Golly!" said Freddie in awe. "I guess we've found the treasure!"

Voices were heard in the garden, and the next

moment the clearing was filled with grown-ups who had come out to see what all the excitement was about. The children ran up to them, all talking together and trying to tell about the fire and their finding the treasure.

Grandma Haarlem, who had insisted on coming down again with the rest, seized her grandson's arm and walked over to the treasure box. The two stood looking down at it in silence for a few moments. Then the old lady said with a tremble in her voice:

"There it is, Grandson, safe and sound after all these long years of searching for it! I could not find it but these dear children have. We owe them a great deal, Frederick."

"We do indeed," said Frederick Haarlem gravely. "It was a lucky day for us when the Bobbsey family came to Windmill Cottage."

"It's really Dykie you should thank," said Nan gaily. "If she hadn't chased the mouse and knocked over the flare that set the mill on fire—"

"We wouldn't have dug in the hole that hid the box that held the treasure," finished Bert with a laugh.

Although everybody agreed that Dykie was a very clever cat, the Haarlems insisted upon giving the major share of the credit to the children.

However, the twins noticed that when Dykie

came up to her mistress in the garden on the way back to the house, the old lady picked up her pet and stroked the soft black fur with unusual gentleness. So Dykie was to come in for her share of the credit, after all!

When they all reached the cottage, Mother Bobbsey called the children to come in to bed. "We have to be up early in the morning, you know," she reminded them, "to be ready for the long ride back to Lakeport."

The children felt as if they never could have such a wonderful time again. They thought this because they did not know about their next vacation. That story is called "The Bobbsey Twins at Lighthouse Point."

"It's too bad we must go home," said Nan, pausing to look longingly about the garden. "We've had such a wonderful time here."

"Well, I don't mind going home half so much, now that we've found the treasure," said Freddie.

The rest of the Bobbsey Twins agreed.

THE END